FOUND2

Eighteen more stories
of found footage horror.

Edited by
Andrew Cull and Gabino Iglesias

Published by Vermillion2One Press 2024.

Cover design and artwork by
Alan Lastufka.

Copy editing by
Noel Osualdini.

FOUND2. More stories of
found footage horror.
Editorial and collection copyright © 2024
Vermillion2One Press.

Individual stories copyright ©
of their respective authors.

ISBN: 978-0-6487315-6-6

Special thanks to:

Kerrie and Team Boo
Gabino
Noel Osualdini
BP Gregory

Everyone who submitted a
story for this anthology. You're
incredibly spooky, in the best way.

You were warned before.
You didn't listen.

Look at what happened.

BURN THIS BOOK.

"FOUND AGAIN"

Gabino Iglesias

We're back! Can you believe it? Oh, this is an awesome thing. Listen, I don't know if Andrew thought we would be back, but I think he did. I even think I know when it happened, when the thought first popped into his head. It was probably right after so many of you picked up the previous edition. That was great, so thank you. But you didn't stop there. No, you read it, too. And then many of you reviewed it and talked about it on social media. Damn. That's almost enough to squeeze a thug tear from the corner of my eye. I'm serious. Your support is why we're here again. Your attention and time and voices mean the world to us, so thank you again.

Okay! That's enough emotional stuff. Let's get to the horror. Ah, there's plenty of it here, and it all exists somewhere on the found footage spectrum. But I don't want this to be a regular introduction, so I'm not going to dissect some stories here and call that an intro. First, I believe the pleasure of slicing open those stories should be all yours. Second, I want to talk about something important here, something exciting that applies to every story in this anthology. I want to talk about how found footage horror is growing and getting more attention.

Fans of the genre know that it's been around for a long time (don't worry, I'm not going to get all academic here). However, many of us came to it when it was still seen as a bad joke or lowbrow art so low it didn't even merit attention. Now, found footage is everywhere. People generally know what it is. We have more and more movies as well as more and more books playing in that sandbox, using that aesthetic. And that last one — aesthetic—is crucial. In many ways, found footage is a style, a look, a feel, an aura, a lens. All those things are relatively easy to communicate in video because the graininess of the image or the shakiness of the camera speak volumes to found footage connoisseurs. Ah, but there's no image, no shakiness, in fiction. In fiction, every story looks the same: words. Those writing found footage fiction must bring that aesthetic, that lens, to the page while also telling us a story. Isn't fiction magic? Anyway, the point is, if you are writing this stuff, you rock. Keep at it.

The second thing I wanted to mention here is that this is an indie publication. Andrew is superhuman. He's the one who makes this happen, and for that we all owe him many thanks. But Andrew—and you, and me, and the next dozen small presses—are small parts of a bigger world, a larger community. As with all other communities, there are many cases of individuals behaving badly. That always gets a lot of attention. And that's good! We should all come together to fight racism, homophobia, harassment, and any other kind of abuse. But sometimes those things eclipse the good things happening in the community. Folks keep selling stories, getting acceptances. New presses managing to make a profit. Authors getting paid on time. Authors finding agents. Little anthologies making waves and getting a second volume. Those things are also out there, and I want you to remember that. This is a good community. Sure, not everyone is good, but most people are, and that's worthy of celebration.

We're back! Thank you for riding with us again. We've brought you stories that speak for themselves. That leave a mark. They found that thing, that tape, that letter, that piece of audio, that security camera footage. It's about to get dark and weird in here. Enjoy.

With love,

Gabino Iglesias
Co-Editor

"THE RED ROOM TAPE"

Andrew Cull

The British film industry has always been rife with superstition and myth. Going back to the days of Hammer, there are stories of cursed sets, haunted actors, people you shouldn't employ, places you shouldn't shoot because they brought bad luck, or worse. When I was working in film and television in London, there were a lot of urban legends that did the rounds of sets and edit suites.

My time behind the camera was (fortunately) curse free. We didn't tempt fate though. After the scene in *The Possession of David O'Reilly* where David uses a glass and a newspaper like a Ouija board, we had a priest visit our set (which was a real house) and carry out a blessing. There are some things you just don't trifle with.

I worked in and around Soho, London, for almost 10 years, so I spent a lot of time with horror people talking (you guessed it) horror[1]. Over those years, though, there was no place I heard more urban legends and ghost stories than I did when I was in edit suites.

Think about it: you're putting a bunch of film buffs and obsessives in a dark room for days on end. We talked *a lot*. One of my favorite stories involved the original audio tapes that Maurice Grosse had recorded at Green Street during the Enfield Poltergeist case. Apparently, there were more tapes than Grosse had allowed to be broadcast. This was because those extra tapes featured graphic descriptions and language that he felt would be inappropriate to share. Remember, he was making these recordings in 1977-79. British society was very different then. More alarmingly, he felt that details in the recordings clearly indicated that the spirit calling itself Bill/Fred was not simply someone who had died in the house but a much darker and more malevolent entity. Grosse was so shaken by these tapes that he'd intended to destroy them. Before he could do that, the tapes were mislaid.

Rumor has it, that those tapes found their way into the hands of an occult collector whose kept them in a locked box in their central London house ever since.

---

[1] In *Did You Forget About Me?* when the Cam Miller talks about his time in London and sharing an elevator with Christopher Lee, that was a true story. Our agents had offices on different floors of the same building. I was far too star-struck to talk to him.

As a teenager, I was a huge fan of Maurice Grosse and his work. Fun fact: I applied to join the Society for Psychical Research when I was thirteen! I think they told me to reapply when I was a bit older. Either way, I would've loved to hear those original recordings, but rumors about their whereabouts (and who that collector was) were as close as I ever got to them.

Another story revolved around The Red Room Tape. The Red Room Tape concerns (you guessed it) a videotape of an entirely red room. The walls are red, the floor is red, and there's a red chair in the center of the shot.

The tape was almost certainly shot on film and converted to video. It may've been colorized, too[2]. It's said to run for up to an hour (the length varies from version to version), and the shot remains the same throughout. According to some, even though the picture doesn't change, the room does.

An experienced TV editor told me the lighting in the room shifts, and shadows grow longer. But the thing is that they also shrink. So, it's not the position of the sun moving. He said it's more like the room is breathing. That stuck with me.

---

[2] Viewers report the red color to be extremely deep. Unnaturally so.

The legend goes that every now and then, The Red Room Tape will turn up. It's been found on movie sets, in edit suites, in at least one actor's home (more on that below). It's not a tape that's supposed to kill you when you watch it, but it's definitely weird and has some distinctly unsettling history associated with it.

There are theories that the Red Room is a room in a private mansion in Berkshire[3], somewhere close to the location of Bray Studios[4], where Hammer Films shot many of their movies in the '50s and '60s. Other versions of the story have it as a film set that was used in a (pre-Vincent Prince) adaptation of *The Masque of the Red Death* that was plagued by disaster, on-set accidents, and finally, a fire that consumed the Red Room itself.

Another version of the story goes that the room was used by Aleister Crowley[5] for rituals and black masses. When I was editing *The Possession of David O'Reilly*, I heard a version of the story that said there was audio on the tape of someone behind the camera sobbing and wailing in Latin.

---

[3] Possibly Oakley Court. 'After its conversion to flats in the late 1960s 'paranormal activity in and around the house intensified to the extent that it became described not only as haunted but evil' (Brian Langston, 'The Real Hammer House of Horror: Oakley Court Hotel Windsor')

[4] https://en.wikipedia.org/wiki/Bray_Film_Studios

[5] Some have suggested that the location of the Red Room may have been Foxhill House in Berkshire. It's only 20 minutes from Bray Studios. See: 'The bizarre story of the University of Reading building that was declared a centre of devil worship' https://www.getreading.co.uk/news/berkshire-history/bizarre-story-university-reading-building-20200211

The voice itself is apparently exceptionally deep. My friend described it as "crawling over him". He was pretty drunk (and stoned) when he saw the tape (back in 2010). The most unsettling part of his recollection of that experience was the way that, for days after, whenever a room fell silent he was sure he could hear the voice.

That editor is still alive and well and working in London. See, watching the tape doesn't kill you! Whenever I talk to him, I ask if he's heard about The Red Room Tape surfacing anywhere. The last time we talked was at the end of 2019, and he told me that he had.

We've both become Red Room Tape enthusiasts over the years, so he keeps an ear out for any stories. We share a love the history of Hammer Films, and it feels that The Red Room Tape ties into that. Often, the stories come from other editors, ADs, and producers he meets.

So, apparently, in June of 2019, a copy of the tape turned up at the home of a young actor (from a long-established acting family) in South London. This actor decided it'd be a good idea to have a screening of the tape at a wrap party for the movie he'd just completed.

On the night of the party, 20 or so drunk guests crammed into a small Soho screening room to watch the tape. For theatrical effect, the actor locked the doors behind them and (get this) swallowed the key before beginning to play the video.

Shortly after the recording began, someone smelled smoke. By the time firefighters arrived, the fire had engulfed the screening room. Fortunately, a security guard had heard the guests yelling and knocking before the fire had taken hold. If he hadn't been passing, the actor's stunt would almost certainly have ended terribly. The Red Room Tape was destroyed in the fire, and my friend said he hadn't heard of any more copies surfacing since. I think he's a bit relieved. His viewing of the tape definitely stayed with him.

Is that the last we'll hear of The Red Room Tape? I'd love to hear more stories about the recording if anyone knows any. Feel free to contact me via Twitter or Instagram with any tips. If nothing else, it's a fascinating urban legend that ties into Hammer Films (which I love) and possibly Occultism. But maybe, just maybe, it's more than that.

I'd planned to write about The Red Room Tape back when I first started thinking about *FOUND*. Then the Boyd Thomas Sinclair case made the news and that became the subject of my introduction to the first book. Urban legends thread through the found footage genre with a natural ease. Both walk the same line between fact and fiction. They overlap. They're whispered in the same breath. Found footage is where horror meets truth and then (quietly) murders it.

The scare that's indistinguishable from the truth is the one that'll keep you up at night. *FOUND2* will keep you up at night. I'd put money on that.

Gabino and I are stoked to be able to bring you eighteen more stories of found footage horror. More transcripts, more VHS tapes, more emails, and more clowns. Long live found footage!

Andy Cull. Melbourne, Australia. Oct '24.

CONTENTS

PLAY>

~~make~~

PLAY>

~~it~~

PLAY>

~~STOP~~

PLAY>

"FOR YOUR CONSIDERATION"

Rhiannon A Grist

Dear Mr Gabino Iglesias and Mr Andy Cull,

My name is Rhiannon, and I'd like to submit my previously unpublished 2,500 word short story "For Your Consideration" to your open call for *FOUND #2: More stories of found footage horror*. I appreciate this is unusual, but the story is in this covering letter. I'll explain why later, but for now let me introduce myself.

I'm a Welsh writer of weird and dark fiction, but I've not always been so attuned to the macabre. In fact, I grew up in an evangelical Christian home near Cardiff. The evangelical church doesn't have the same stranglehold over Britain as it does the United States, so it was a pretty isolating upbringing — especially when it came to music.

While my classmates were listening to Steps, BoyZone, The Spice Girls, Oasis and Blur, the only "approved" music I could listen to came from contemporary Christian bands like DC Talk, Delirious?, Phatfish and The World Wide Message Tribe. Even when I was younger, as other kids sang "Wheels on the Bus," I was singing "I'm in the Lord's Army (Yes sir!)" complete with salutes and rifle poses.

As you might imagine, I wasn't the most popular kid. I didn't do myself any favors, either. On my first day of secondary school, during introductions in my new registration class, I stood up and declared that I loved the Lord Jesus Christ with all my heart. I took the awkward pause from the teacher, and the quiet titters that rippled around me, as a mark of pride. I told myself I was doing it for Him, but these days I see it more for the cop-out it was. The pastor of my church took great pleasure in telling me how the world would reject me for my faith. I think that cringey announcement was just my way of getting ahead of the world. Most of my registration class just gave me a wide berth, but Kelly Morgan made my life a living hell.

She'd kick my chair out as I'd go to sit in it. She threw my bag in dirty puddles. She even once spat on me, full-throated, from the top floor of the school double decker bus as I went walking by.

I don't know why Kelly took such a personal interest in my punishment. At the time I thought it was religious persecution like my pastor had promised. These days I think she just had her own problems and I was an easy target, a place to put her rage that would never fight back. God help me, the first time she hit me I actually turned the other cheek. Then she punched me again. I quickly learned the better response was to wrap my arms around my head and try and wait it out.

I really believed back then I was suffering for God. Stupid kid.

You might be wondering why I'm telling you all this. It's because I need you to understand why I didn't immediately spot anything wrong. Growing up, declaring undying love and loyalty to an unseen force wasn't just entirely normal, it was encouraged. I would regularly sing songs with lyrics along the lines of "I want to see your kingdom come" or "take my life, my soul" or "less of me, more of you oh Lord". And some with lyrics glorifying the destruction of some enemy. "No weapon forged against me shall prosper." "Nothing shall stand against you."

So, when I found ██████████████████ [6] it sounded just like any other contemporary pop-rock single coming from the various Christian bands at the time.

It was on the free CD attached to an issue of *Cross Rhythms*—the go-to Christian music magazine at the time. As with secular music magazines, these compilations were a common promotional tactic for new bands looking to grow their audience. One of the bands on this issue was called Lord of All—a

---

[6] Editors' note: In the interests of public safety, we have redacted the song title.

fairly standard band name at the time—and they had a track called ██████████████. It was catchy, if a little strange. It had an odd melody, but I enjoyed the challenge of trying to follow it as I sang along. The lyrics were also—in my experience—fairly standard, if a little more aggressive than usual. Normally, Christian rock tracks either profess love for Christ—famously you can replace the word "Jesus" with "Baby" and make most a standard love song—or ask for defense against malevolent forces trying to turn the listener away from God.

This one called for their active destruction:

You alone are my strength (my strength) and my sword (my sword)

You can stop my enemies (my enemies) with a single word (your word)

I wanna see them run before you (ooh ooh) I wanna see them turn (yeah yeah)

Avenge me oh Lord (my Lord) Make my enemies burn (burn burn)

The chorus was one of those archaic names for God sung over and over. I was used to contemporary Christian songs littering their lyrics with somewhat ignorantly lifted Hebrew, Latin or Aramaic terms. In Sunday worship I'd regularly find myself calling God *Elohim, El Shaddai, Yahweh, Jehovah* or *Abba Father.* I just assumed the name I sang in the chorus of ██████████████ was a similar deal.

It took a little while for me to get the song down, but after a few weeks of humming it on the bus or singing it in the shower, I could soon belt it out without even thinking about it. On a particularly disastrous day at school (Kelly got her older sister to pour a whole two liter bottle of Fanta over my head between classes) I found myself quietly singing it as I tried to wash my sticky hair in the girls' bathroom.

Avenge me oh Lord. Make my enemies burn.

The next day Kelly wasn't at school. My registration teacher told us there had been an accident behind the bike sheds — the place her sister usually went to smoke. The police weren't sharing the details, but they thought she and the other smokers must have been playing with aerosols. The other smokers denied it, of course.

When Kelly came back to school a few weeks later, she was…different. Quieter. The teachers were softer on her, even when she refused to do any work in class. All throughout the day, though, I felt her eyes burning into the back of my head. I tried to get a head start on the walk home, but it didn't take long for her and her friends to catch up with me. I tried to lose them by taking a different route through town, but between roadworks and my complete lack of street smarts — I wasn't allowed out on the weekends: too many temptations, according to my mum — I ended up stuck in a dead-end between the Woolworths and Boots. Before I could backtrack, Kelly and her friends blocked off the alley. As she advanced, I found myself squeezing my eyes tight, singing that song, praying God would save me. I imagine Kelly must have been thrilled to see me reduced to a gibbering wreck, to see me pray for help as she approached me.

But then my god answered.

There was a whoosh and then this simmering wave of warmth.

I opened my eyes.

Kelly was glowing!

She lit up the alley in a heavenly light. Her skin was incandescent.

And then it was blistering.

And then it was burning.

Cracks spread up her arms. Her flesh blackened and split. Her eyes melted out of her head. Her mouth distended and an awful, inhuman scream echoed off the walls. She stumbled helplessly in stupid panicky circles as her awful little friends looked on in horror.

It took me a week to wash the smell of her out of my hair.

Once again, the police blamed aerosol misuse: little sister mimicking big sister. School got a lot better after that. I still didn't have many friends, but no one bullied me anymore.

That was the first time I made the connection. I looked at the world with a new perspective. At church, I realized the same people went up for prayer week after week, asking for divine aid for the same things each time. Money. Love. Family. Health. But nothing ever changed. Every week, the same people made the same pleas. And every week, their pleas would go unanswered. I'd never noticed it before, but now it was glaringly obvious. If there was a God, he wasn't listening to them. Meanwhile, the prayers I made while singing that song kept getting answered.

I decided to find out why.

I couldn't find any information about the band Lord of All. Aside from that one song, they never put out any other music. Even the names of the band members came to a dead end. It was as if they'd never existed.

I turned to theology. But all I found were vague platitudes about God's will, faith and that gumph about only giving us the trials he knows we can handle.

So, I branched out a little further. Kabbalah. Theosophy. Hermeticism.

After many years of googling and reading, I finally found myself on the Aspects of Near-Eastern Demonology short course at Edinburgh University. Between the ancient monsters and the forgotten gods, I discovered something very interesting. People used to believe the main difference between a demon and a god is that gods require tributes if you want to gain their favor—sacrifices, prayers, pledges of life and loyalty. But demons can be trapped. This goes beyond the apotropaic sigils of folk magic and the early church. Apparently, King Solomon tricked a demon into servitude and made it build the First Temple of Jerusalem. Other schools of belief advise the user to show at least a modicum of politeness if you don't want the entrapped entity to turn on you upon its inevitable release.

One method of entrapment is the use of a magic square. You know what magic squares are, right? Those puzzles where you fit the same words vertically and diagonally, like the famous Sator Square or — perhaps more relevantly — the twelve-by-twelve magic square found in *The Book of Sacred Magic of Abramelin the Mage*. In ancient times, people would use them as charms for healing or protection. Something about the repeated words, the math of it, could trap a demon wishing you harm or a miasma passing on the wind. They could even summon a demon you wished to enlist to your aid. The Mesopotamians didn't even need to draw the square. They believed you could invoke the spell by simply repeating the words over and over.

This immediately made me think of the song's strange melody. I'm not the most musically gifted, but with a little googling, I found a tool that translated the music in the audio file into a written format. That's when I saw it:

A	B	Bm	A	D
B	A	B	D	A
Bm	B	A	B	A
A	D	B	A	B
D	A	A	B	Bm

The chorus forms a magic square, only instead of words it's chord sequences. I must have run the music through the program a hundred times, and each time it came back the same. Seeing that first line though, the one that would traditionally give the square its title, froze me to my chair. I recognized it immediately. You see, it spelled out something similar to the name sung over and over in the chorus. The name I thought was another ancient title for God, like "Abba Father."

     A   B   Bm   A   D
     ABBAD
     Abba Don

It was what I'd been singing for years, over and over, on the toilet, on my walks, through my tears, in my rage.

     Ah-bba Don. Abba Don.
     Ah-bba Don. Abba Don.
     Ah-bba Don. Abba Don.
     Ah-bah-ah Doh-on
     Make my enemies burn.

I'm not going to insult your intelligence. I think you can see by now that I wasn't singing to God. And it wasn't God avenging me.

Maybe you'd assume, after learning this, I would have stopped singing ████████████████.

But I haven't.

If anything, I now sing it a little more…selectively.

I sang it after my lecherous neighbor made a drunken pass at me. I sang it at work when Andy was given my most-coveted client. I sang it on my way to the British Fantasy Awards which, luckily for the organizers, I won.

Turning the other cheek never worked. Why give up the one thing that did?

Hell, I even sang it this morning at my desk when I submitted this story to you.

Which finally brings us to why this is a covering letter.

I'm of the opinion that good found footage horror should always come with a sliver of believability, the potential that what you're seeing—or in this case, reading—might be true. Which is why I had to tell you all of this in the covering letter and not within the safe bounds of a story. Because the covering letter is supposed to be the part that isn't fiction. This is the part that's *supposed* to be true.

And now the next part of this story is up to you.

Ok, let's be real for a moment. Demons don't *really* exist, right? There are no records of spontaneous combustion from my hometown. And there'd probably be a considerably longer trail of bodies in my wake if all this were true. This is probably just another weird story from sweet, dorky Rhiannon. Always singing her funny little songs.

Or maybe it is the truth, and I really am admitting to brutally burning my enemies alive—whomever I perceive them to be at the time.

There's only one way to find out.

Say "no" to this story.

Send the form rejection, the *thanks but no thanks*, the *I hope it finds a home elsewhere*. Then cross your fingers and wait. Or include it and admit to yourselves—and everyone reading this right now—

that a little part of you, not a lot perhaps but just enough, is afraid that I might be telling the truth.

Like I said, up to you.

I appreciate this story has been a little different from what you might have been expecting, but I think you'll understand its value. If not, I'm confident I'll survive my disappointment.

I'm not sure the same could be said for you, though.

Or your contributors for that matter.

Thanks in advance for your consideration. I'm sure you'll make the right choice.

Yours in faith,
Rhiannon A Grist

EMANCIPATION

A Research Guide for a North Dakota Civil Court Process

The North Dakota Legal Self Help Center provides resources to people who represent themselves in civil matters in the North Dakota state courts.

The information provided in this research guide is intended as a starting point for your research into Emancipation. The information provided in this research guide is **not** intended for legal advice and **cannot** replace the advice of competent legal counsel licensed in the state.

The self-represented individual must make all decisions about how to proceed.

References to non-ND Legal Self Help Center resources are included for your convenience only. Including these references does not mean the ND Legal Self Help Center endorses, warrants, or accepts responsibility for the content or uses of the resource. Use at your own risk.

OVERVIEW OF EMANCIPATION:

What is emancipation?

The act of allowing a minor child to gain independence and take on the full responsibilities of an adult.

What is the age of majority?

The age of majority in North Dakota is 18 years of age, meaning at the age of 18 a minor child has reached the age of an adult and is no longer under the authority of the parent.

Emancipation by a North Dakota court prior to reaching the age of majority?

North Dakota does not have an established civil court process to ask a state court to emancipate a minor child.

When does a parent's authority over a child end?

- After reaching the age of majority.
- When the minor child is married before the age of majority (with parental consent).
- When a court appoints a guardian for the minor child.

What can a minor do without parental consent?

- Work
- Consent to SOME medical treatments
- Enter into many, but not all, contracts
- Bring suit (may sue or be sued)

Daily Dako[ta]

Lyndsay Hash Found Alive

Lyndsay Lynette Hash was last seen seven years ago, the day before her mother and father were found brutally slain in their Bismarck home. Dakotans never gave up hope for the little girl's safe return, and yesterday, just one day after her 18th birthday, Hash was found alive.

An anonymous tip led the FBI to a garage two blocks off W. Stutsman St in Pembina, Nd. Inside, agents recovered Hash, who they claim appeared to have been imprisoned against her will. According to Bismarck Police, Stephen Arthur Griggs, 55, a local mechanic for hire in Pembina, owns the home.

It had been theorized that Hash's parents were slain by the serial killer known as "February Fred," a moniker used due to the timing and violent nature of his murders, which have been described as akin to villain Freddy Krueger's in A Nightmare on Elm Street.

Griggs is being held on state kidnapping charges in Bismarck while the FBI's investigation of the February Fred case is ongoing. Details about that federal investigation remain scarce

File Number: ███ ND-2173732
Recording Name: 170603_01.WAV

UNITED STATES DEPARTMENT OF JUSTICE FEDERAL BUREAU OF INVESTIGATION

Source File Information   June 13, 2022
170603 01.WAV

VERBATIM TRANSCRIPTION

Participants:

SAT	**Special Agent Christine Throne**
SAP	**Special Agent David Paxton**
SAG	**Stephen Arthur Griggs**

SAT: This is my partner, David Paxton… Okay if he joins?

SAG: (inaudible)

SAT: Mr. Griggs, I'm told you've been advised of your rights and are still willing to speak to us without a lawyer present. Can you give verbal confirmation this is correct?

SAG: That is correct.

SAT: And you are aware that this conversation is being recorded, correct?

SAG: Yes.

SAT: Lucky me, I guess.

SAG: Lucky you, indeed. I doubt you'll ever have it easier than me.

SAT: How so?

SAG: At some point, I'll be ready to confess, of course… on my terms.

SAT: Confess to what?

SAG: All of it. All of *them*.

SAT: *Them*, Mr. Griggs?

SAG: Oh… we can talk about the young woman you "saved" first if you like.

SAT: You are talking about Lyndsay Lynette Hash.

SAG: Yes. Ms. Hash. After all, she's the only one still alive… and free.

SAT: You sound upset.

SAG: You all puppy dogs and rainbows when someone stabs you in the back?

[cont]

•••○○ Sprint LTE   4:08 PM
< Messages   Gabs

Y weren't u at school today?

Sick

FR sick?

Y

U r sick a lot Lynz

Dad's fault

Ur dad sick 2?

Not in way you think.

What do you mean?

Shit. I gotta go

both those assholes are screaming about something downstairs. TTYL

B Kerful luv U

BURLEIGH COUNTY SHERIFF'S OFFICE

BURLEIGH COUNTY SHERIFF'S OFFICE, FEBRUARY 5, 2015 (10:30 A.M.)

The following is a statement of Deputy David J. Holmes, age 32, with reference to the investigation of the homicides of Matthew William Hash, age 48, and Vera Katherine Hash, age 45, address 1444 Portland Dr. Bismarck, North Dakota, 58504.

I am a duly appointed member of the Burleigh County Sheriff's Department and am assigned to regular duty.

On Wednesday afternoon of February 1, 2015, I received a dispatch concerning a telephone call to 9-1-1 made at 5:34 P.M. A male voice stated, "I think something unavoidable has happened to the Hashes at 1444 Portland Dr." The caller hung up. When no one picked up at the number registered to their home, I told Deputy Edward Vickers to take the other cruiser and follow me. Vickers mentioned "February Fred," and while the same thought had crossed my mind, I did not respond.

It was 7 degrees outside, and the sun was setting when we arrived at the Hash's home. I first noticed all the front exterior windows were open, and both floors had all the lights on. I recalled having read about something similar to that fact in descriptions of the previous homicides thought to have been committed by the serial killer commonly known as February Fred. I asked Deputy Vickers to cover the back side of the home as I approached the front door.

Through the open window to the left of the front door, I saw Mr. Hash's legs sticking out from the television side of the couch in the living room. I asked aloud if he needed help. When there was no response, I shouted for Vickers to meet me inside the home. Vickers entered through the rear door, which he said had also been left open.

Mrs. Hash's body was on the couch. I observed many deep and lengthy lacerations across her face, spanning forehead to chin and ear to ear. [cont]

Case Number: 010004   02/18/2015

Mr. Hash was face down in a pool of blood and, like Mrs. Hash, appeared to be dead at that time. Making an observation of the room, I observed numerous family photos of Mr. and Mrs. Hash with a little girl of various ages, the oldest appearing to be age ten or so. The little girl was later identified as Lyndsay Lynette Hash, 11.

After radioing for EMS to be sent immediately, I contacted Bismarck Chief of Police Roger Stanton and Sgt. Tom Doyle. As they made their way to the Hash residence, Vickers and I searched the home and the property for what we presumed to be Mr. and Mrs. Hash's daughter. Though we found spots of blood as we searched, there was no clear indication that their daughter might have also been a victim at that time.

During our search, we observed an older security system housed in the Master Bedroom Closet. The pattern in the dust on the shelving next to the two monitors suggested that there had been numerous VHS tapes on the shelves at one time. There was also no tape in the recorder/player, and only after this discovery did I note that each room in the house had at least one camera mounted to an interior corner.

When EMS and Roger Stanton arrived, I was asked to place a call to Mayor Donald Williams to inform him about the situation. With Homicide on the way, it was decided that I should set up and enforce the press perimeter. On my way out, I overheard Deputy Edward Vickers tell Chief Stanton that Mr. Hash had been disemboweled and that a foreign object resembling a child's stuffed teddy bear had been jammed into the cavity. To my knowledge, that detail did not match previous accounts of kills performed by FF. It struck me as odd. Regardless of the peculiarity and my passing thoughts about it, many reporters outside had already begun broadcasting live and calling the scene another February Fred massacre. I noted to myself that if FF had committed the murders, it was possible that he was escalating the violence of his kills and had decided to add disembowelment and the child's toy to keep things interesting.

Reporting Officer: _______________________   DATE: 2-15

Sworn to and subscribed before me this 5 day of 2 2015   Total Pages: 2 of 2

CRIMINAL DISTRICT COURT
BURLEIGH COUNTY
STATE OF NORTH DAKOTA

STATE OF NORTH DAKOTA
NO. 123-456
VERSUS
      SECTION "B"
STEPHEN ARTHUR GRIGGS

Trial Hearing

Testimony and Notes of Evidence, taken in the above-entitled and numbered case, before the **HON. LAWRENCE HOLDER**, Judge, presiding on the 8th day of November, 2022.

APPEARANCES:
    REPRESENTING THE STATE OF NORTH DAKOTA:
    LISA DAVENPORT – ASSISTANT DISTRICT ATTORNEY

    REPRESENTING THE DEFENDANT:
    STEPHEN ARTHUR GRIGGS – DEFENDANT

REPORTED BY:
    SALLY HANCOCK
    OFFICIAL COURT REPORTER
    IN AND FOR THE COUNTY OF BURLEIGH
    STATE OF NORTH DAKOTA

PROCEEDING INDEX

                      PAGE

MS. DAVENPORT:

Your honor, the State is ready to proceed.

MR. GRIGGS:

Your honor, myself on behalf of myself.

THE COURT:

This is the matter of the *State versus Stephen Arthur Griggs.*

MR. GRIGGS:

Yes. I am present in court, as you can see, and I'm ready to proceed.

THE COURT:

Very well. Ms. Davenport, you may proceed with your cross examination of Mr. Griggs.

- CROSS EXAMINATION –

BY MS. DAVENPORT:

Q.   Could you please state your name for the record?

A.   Stephen Arthur Griggs. AKA February Fred… some say anyway.

Q.   Actually, you have said, Mr. Griggs. Yesterday, in fact, under your own direct examination.

A.   Just trying to be modest. Hi Lyndsay.

MS. DAVENPORT:

Your honor, if it pleases the court, I'd ask that Mr. Griggs not address the victim directly while under cross examination.

THE COURT:

Mr. Griggs, the same warning I gave yesterday applies. You are not to address Ms. Hash directly while under cross examination or at any other time in my courtroom.

MS. DAVENPORT:

Thank you, your honor.

MR. GRIGGS:

Understood, your honor.

Q. Mr. Griggs, yesterday you testified under your own direct examination that you murdered Matthew and Vera Hash, Lyndsay's parents.

A. I did.

Q. Thereafter, you also admitted to having murdered 56 other persons between the years 1998 and 2021. Is that correct?

A. It is.

Q. And yet you also denied having kidnapped Ms. Hash. Testifying that "the living situation was a mutual decision made by me and Ms. Hash." Is that also correct?

A. That's what it was.

Q. We know that's what you believe it was, Mr. Griggs. Besides your testimony yesterday, what evidence can you offer to the court to prove that you didn't kidnap Ms. Hash after killing her parents?

A. Just find the tapes.

Q. Are the tapes you are referring to the supposed Hash Home Security tapes you claimed yesterday will show that Ms. Hash went with you willingly?

A. Yes.

Q. You also testified you never harmed or hurt Ms. Hash. If I were to ask you the same today—have you ever physically or sexually assaulted Ms. Hash—would you claim the same?

A. I would. Bring me in again tomorrow, and I'll say it again: I never harmed a hair on that girl's head. Never touched her—sexually or otherwise—took care of her like my own.

Q. Have you had experience taking care of your own children? Did you also lock them up in a garage as a part of caring for them?

A. I've never had any children. It was just an expression.

Q. Is it your intent to claim ignorance regarding child-rearing?

A. That is not my intent. No. The arrangement—her being in the garage and away from me—was the only suitable one.

Q. Suitable to whom?

A. Us both.

Q. She was afraid of you?

A. Couldn't say.

Q. According to your testimony yesterday, you were afraid of Ms. Hash.

A. Not afraid—cautious around. I believe I called it a precaution.

Q. With regard to the kidnapping, the charge we're trying here today in this courtroom, you've pled not guilty. Yet yesterday, with regard to the other two charges—the vile, brutal, and unimaginable murders of Lyndsay's parents—you changed your plea under your own direct examination.

A. I did.

1 Q.   You do understand that you are already going away forever, Mr. Griggs?

2 A.   I do. No shame there because I did do those things.

   Q.   This is an unusual ask, I'll admit, but you are an unusual man. Any chance you'll be changing your not-guilty plea to the charge of kidnapping

4 today?

   A.   No chance.

5 Q.   And why is that?

   A.   Because the woman in this courtroom is lying.

6 Q.   You are referring to Ms. Hash?

   A.   Yes. Though not directly, as the court so graciously asked. She's

7 playing all of you.

   Q.   An insanity defense isn't likely to make much difference now, Mr.

8 Griggs, if that is your intent. It's cut and dry—

9 A.   The evidence you've presented, and even my guilty plea to the murders, will almost assuredly result in the jury finding me guilty of

10 kidnapping. I understand. I'm not playing insane.

   Q.   So, why are we here? It wasn't enough that you took, by your own

11 count and admission, 58 souls and destroyed the lives of countless friends and family? The blood—the unconscionable way in which you ended each

12 and every one of those lives—wasn't enough? You needed one last public spectacle. Killing Ms. Hash's parents and imprisoning her for what

13 remained of her childhood wasn't enough. You decided to take advantage of our legal system to sully her good name by accusing her… well… If

14 I'm being honest, what is it you're trying to say about Ms. Hash?

15 A.   (no response)

16 THE COURT:

       Mr. Griggs, please answer the question.

17 A.   (no response)

18

   THE COURT:

19   Mr. Griggs, are you alright? Mr. Griggs? Mr. Griggs?
       Bailiff, call EMS. Are you having a stroke, Mr. Griggs?

20   Counsel, please return to your seat.

21

   Q.   Sorry about that. I'm alright. I'm alright, and I heard the question,

22 but I've had a change of heart. I am now prepared to change my plea to guilty on all charges relating to the abduction and kidnapping of

23 Ms. Hash. She wins. I figure I always knew she would.

24

   THE COURT:
       The court calls an emergency recess. Counsel, see me in my office.

Daily Dakota

November 9, 2022

GRIGGS' TRIAL ENDS WITH ABRUPT GUILTY PLEA

By M.J. JEROME

After weeks of threatening to "expose the truth" about Lyndsay Lynette Hash's "so-called abduction," Stephen Arthur Griggs, AKA February Fred, changed his plea on a kidnapping charge during cross examination to guilty. Griggs' sudden reversal came on the heels of his freezing up for 11 seconds, during which time District Judge Lawrence Holder asked if Griggs was having a stroke and instructed the bailiff to phone emergency medical services.

When Griggs came to, he abruptly reversed course, informing the court that he "had a change of heart," and then he immediately changed his plea. After restoring order to the courtroom, Judge Holder called an emergency recess. Sometime thereafter, Holder adjourned the trial and scheduled a Tuesday, November 15 sentencing hearing. The abrupt end to the trial was met with raucous applause inside and outside of the Burleigh County Courthouse.

Against the wishes of extended family and public opinion, The Burleigh County D.A.'s office had intended to put Lyndsay Lynette Hash on the stand today, November 9, 2022, to testify in detail on how she came to be Griggs' prisoner after the brutal murder of her parents, one of many homicides that Griggs admitted to during his own direct examination the first day of the trial.

Many psychologists had gone to the airwaves to state their concerns about the long-term effects a possible cross-examination by Griggs, who had been acting as his own counsel, would have on Hash and her recovery from the nearly eight-year ordeal. In the end, Hash's testimony was unnecessary. Both Hash and her counsel declined to comment on Griggs' courtroom incident and his decision to change his pleas.

Reuters

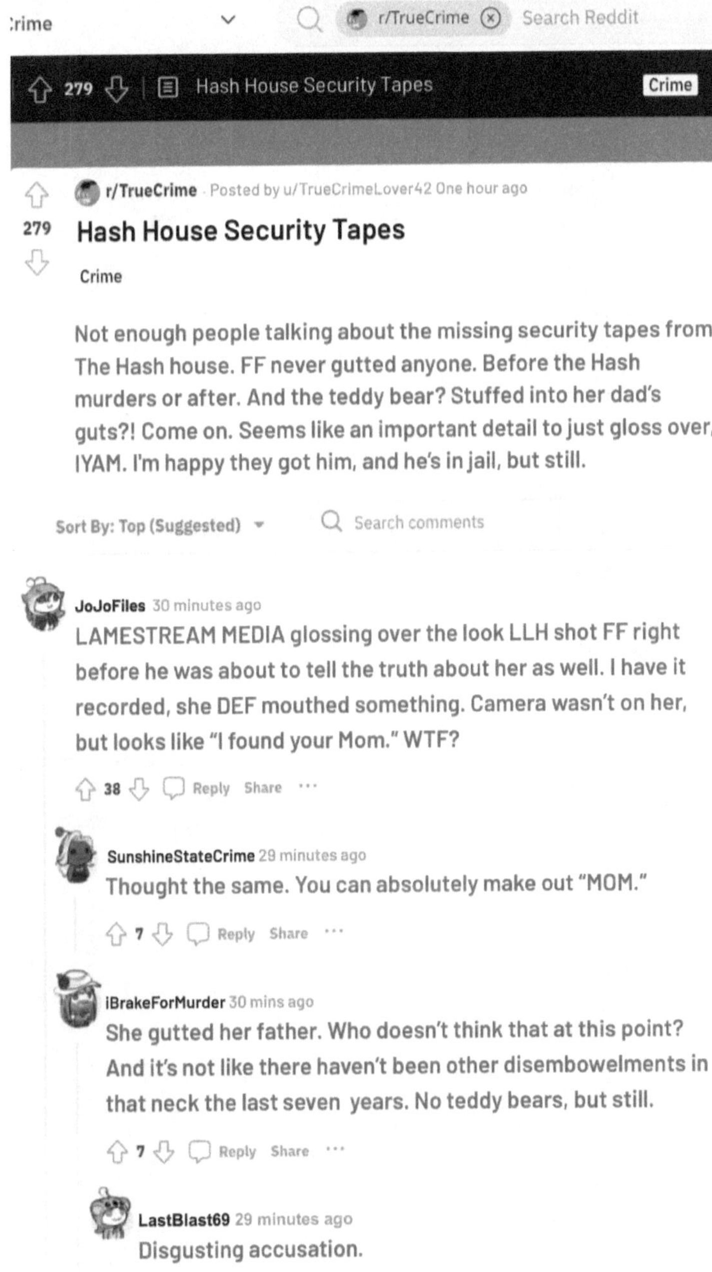

:rime
r/TrueCrime
Search Reddit
279
Hash House Security Tapes
Crime
r/TrueCrime · Posted by u/TrueCrimeLover42 One hour ago
279
Hash House Security Tapes
Crime
Not enough people talking about the missing security tapes from The Hash house. FF never gutted anyone. Before the Hash murders or after. And the teddy bear? Stuffed into her dad's guts?! Come on. Seems like an important detail to just gloss over, IYAM. I'm happy they got him, and he's in jail, but still.
Sort By: Top (Suggested)
Search comments
JoJoFiles 30 minutes ago
LAMESTREAM MEDIA glossing over the look LLH shot FF right before he was about to tell the truth about her as well. I have it recorded, she DEF mouthed something. Camera wasn't on her, but looks like "I found your Mom." WTF?
38   Reply   Share   ···
SunshineStateCrime 29 minutes ago
Thought the same. You can absolutely make out "MOM."
7   Reply   Share   ···
iBrakeForMurder 30 mins ago
She gutted her father. Who doesn't think that at this point? And it's not like there haven't been other disembowelments in that neck the last seven years. No teddy bears, but still.
7   Reply   Share   ···
LastBlast69 29 minutes ago
Disgusting accusation.
2   Reply   Share   ···

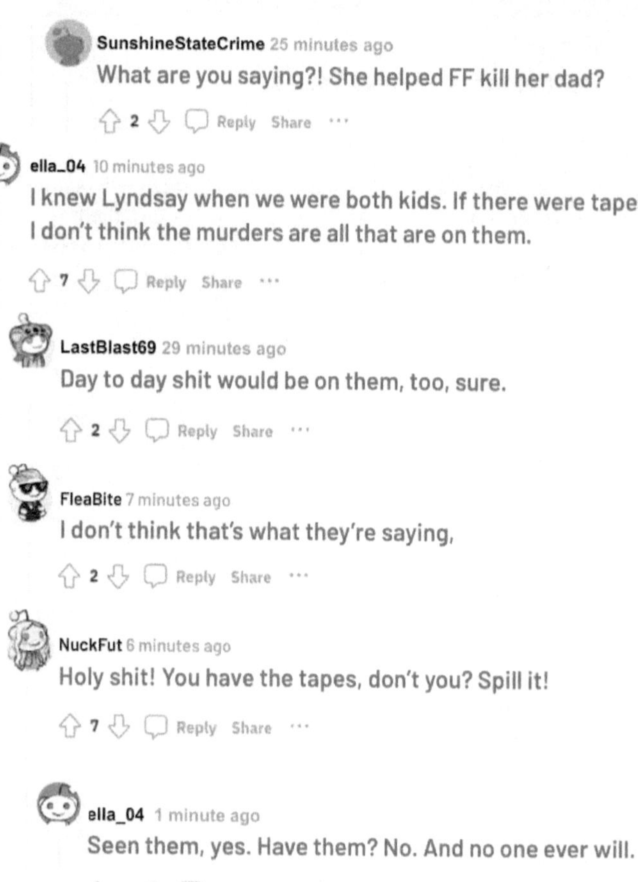
SunshineStateCrime 25 minutes ago
What are you saying?! She helped FF kill her dad?
2 Reply Share
ella_04 10 minutes ago
I knew Lyndsay when we were both kids. If there were tapes, I don't think the murders are all that are on them.
7 Reply Share
LastBlast69 29 minutes ago
Day to day shit would be on them, too, sure.
2 Reply Share
FleaBite 7 minutes ago
I don't think that's what they're saying,
2 Reply Share
NuckFut 6 minutes ago
Holy shit! You have the tapes, don't you? Spill it!
7 Reply Share
ella_04 1 minute ago
Seen them, yes. Have them? No. And no one ever will.
38 Reply Share

Daily Dakot

Wednesday, February 2nd 2023

February Gutter Claims 18t

Charles Duncan White was found dead in his rural Bismarck home yesterday. White was on parole after serving only ten years of a 17-year sentence for the continuous sexual abuse of a child, his own daughter, between the ages of 6 and 10.

After seeing the home's windows open, a neighbor decided to check in on Mr. White. The neighbor, who only met with this reporter on the condition of anonymity, described Mr. White's body as having been torn open from the genitals to just below his sternum. The injuries to Mr. White's body match those often attributed to the serial killer The February Gutter, who some claim to be a copycat killer to the convicted serial murderer Stephen Arthur Griggs. Despite the generally accepted theory that the February Gutter targets only perpetrators of sexual abuse against minors, they have evaded capture by authorities since their first known kill in 2016.

"CLOWN SHOWER"

Caleb Bethea

Have you ever rinsed off in the clown shower?

No.

Have you ever rinsed off in the clown shower?

No, but my best friend growing up did. Said he liked to sit on the purple clown shoes while the water poured over him.

Have you ever rinsed off in the clown shower?

Ah, fuck off.

Have you ever rinsed off in the clown shower?

Yes.

Have you ever rinsed off in the clown shower?

Only because my doctor recommended it. Couldn't explain it with any sort of medical knowledge and she asked me not to share it. But something about his face, I mean, its water helped with my skin condition. Totally cleansed it. I wouldn't do it just for fun. But, it was kinda nice.

Have you ever rinsed off in the clown shower?

I was drunk, okay? My friends dared me to do it. You know how it's sorta way back in the corner of that warehouse? Well, they dared me to strip down at the lockers, which are by the regular shower, and pretty damn far away from the clown shower. But, I was drunk and sweaty. So I got naked and hauled ass, literally, across the warehouse space until I collapsed underneath the clown. I turned the handle on his belt as I caught my breath and I sobered up in that water real quick. I stayed longer than I would have expected, though.

Have you ever rinsed off in the clown shower?

I have, but I don't want to talk about it.

Have you ever rinsed off in the clown shower?

My pastor always said there was something going on in that warehouse, that you shouldn't even go there to lift weights or take an aerobics class, and I believe him.

Have you ever rinsed off in the clown shower?

You asked me the same question yesterday. My answer is the same now as it was then.

Have you ever rinsed off in the clown shower?

Wouldn't you like to know? Bet you get off on that sort of thing. Grimy little pervert.

Have you ever rinsed off in the clown shower?

Before I was saved, I used to go to the warehouse and have a little bit too much fun. We brought our drinks and our smokes and we'd party in the clown shower. It was foolish. And I wouldn't do it again. The way those big plexiglass eyes watch you. It's like your every move is being written in some clown book for all to read. All your mistakes. Right there for some clown to read to himself. And you know he's laughing at you. It's hateful. And wrong. A man's mistakes are his own business. His own mess to clean up.

Have you ever rinsed off in the clown shower?

My ex said he fucked someone in the shower. Apparently, you can almost forget where you are if the sex is good enough. Not sure I believe that, though. I could never have sex in that colorful sort of a setting, the yellow pants, the purple vest. It makes my skin feel lit up, and—you know—observed. I swear, I had to shower in there one time and it was like every layer of my skin was about to fall or float off of me. But the steam just kept massaging it back into place, holding me together in the heat. I feel kinda guilty saying this but I actually kinda liked it. But, I would never…have sex in there. The colors…

Have you ever rinsed off in the clown shower?

My pastor said he did when he was young. And, he saw something in the steam. Hilariously, that's part of what scared him straight to God. He said he should have never been there to begin with, and that God rescued him from many such places.

Have you ever rinsed off in the clown shower?

You know, they told me about you. And I was hoping you'd ask. I've done it. A good handful of times. With a good handful of people. I mean, we weren't naked or anything. Just my swimming trunks. Cigars too. And, god damn, we'd get lightheaded in that thing. We'd light up until the stogies were too soggy to even hold together. By that time, we were spinning around on the floor. Like we were fucking breakdancing or something. Striking poses. Climbing on each other's shoulders to lock lips with the clown. The water spouting out of his mouth and into ours. And there was this guy. It was his first time, having fun, letting off steam. The whole deal. And we lifted him up so he could lay one on the clown's mouth. But, next thing you know, bam! I got so fucking lightheaded that I dropped the kid. Slapped the ridge of his eyebrow right on the tiles. Blood flowering up around his face. When he woke up a few minutes later, he coughed up a tooth and said something about the big clown sitting on his chest with his yellow pants. Kept saying, "He's so heavy. So heavy on my chest." Over and over until we knocked him back out. I don't go there too much anymore. But I'll still rinse off sometimes. By myself.

Have you ever rinsed off in the clown shower?

I don't know what you're talking about, but I wish I did.

Have you ever rinsed off in the clown shower?

Hi. You know, we've never spoken but I've seen you around here before. You have a beautiful way of putting people at ease. I'm not sure I understand your question, but people seem to be drawn to it. Have you ever thought about using your gifts for another purpose? Have you ever considered sharing the good news? So many people just clam up the second they have to talk about Christ. But someone like you, you could start such wonderful conversations. Now, I'm not sure if you know Jesus Christ or not. But, you don't have to preach about him if you're worried about that. No need. Evangelism is more of a dialogue than anything, an exchange. And it's one of our last lines of defense against the dark forces. In times like these, it's easy to see that the enemy is smiling at all the chaos he's created. And it's of eternal importance that we're washed clean by the blood of Jesus.

Have you ever rinsed off in the clown shower?

Sorry, I don't talk to guys who put tiny microphones in my face.

Have you ever rinsed off in the clown shower?

You know, I actually used to work in the warehouse, but I never used the clown shower. We pretty much stayed as far away as we could unless we were ordered to go clean up the aftermath or something. It wasn't that bad to be honest, but the worst part was the smell. That part was terrible. We couldn't ever connect it to what we were cleaning off the floor or the walls or the face of the clown. But, you know those smells that are burnt up in your memory and they immediately take you back to your childhood? Well, it was like that. But, it was only things you would never want to remember. Things that never happened. Even shit that's yet to come.

Have you ever rinsed off in the clown shower?

If you're going to keep asking me that and not remember when I tell you no, then I guess I'm just going to have to make some shit up for you to shut the hell up, huh? Yes, I rinsed off in the clown shower. It was hot. I was terrified. The colors all blurred together into one crushing weight on my chest. The water became the blood inside me. I was possessed with the joy of a clown. Made new. Made whole. Is that good enough? Or do you want me to go on about how I felt like I was getting saved and going to hell all at once? Like I was in the heat of purgatory itself. Crying my goddamn eyes out at the feet of a clown. And all you know now is how easy it is to come completely undone. Looking at a lifeless, painted face. Coming absolutely fucking undone.

Have you ever rinsed off in the clown shower?

I'm more of a bath person. You know when you've just been in there soaking for an hour and your toes are covered in these wet skin canyons–that's what I call them anyway. And you pour a whole bottle of soap into the water just to feel a little something more. But, the bath's running cold and you turn the handle all the way to the left. It burns you. But, a part of you likes it… Yes, I've been to the clown shower.

Have you ever rinsed off in the clown shower?

I said, fuck off. The fuck is wrong with you?

Have you ever rinsed off in the clown shower?

My best friend's dad was a deacon in our church. And my friend and I were normal kids, partying, cutting up. But, since his dad was high up in the church, I'd always have to go sneak him out of his window. One of the things we liked to do most was go to the bonfire Saturday night. Well, I started to realize that when I was driving him back home, his dad was pulling into the driveway around the same time. Wouldn't have been super weird on its own—maybe he was getting the church ready for Sunday service, I don't know. But he was always wearing a bathrobe and his hair was all slicked wet against his dome. You can probably see where I'm going with this. It was like he'd just hopped out of the shower. So, it didn't take too many of those Saturday nights before we decided to follow him to where he was going.

We borrowed a friend's car so we could tail him. Sure enough, he pulled up to the warehouse. A bunch of meatheads were getting into their cars while a bunch of our church elders were getting out of theirs. Lots of hugging and laughing between the elders, and the meatheads were basically crashing into each other trying to get out of that parking lot. And we smoked some blacks while we waited—got through a whole pack and were about to puke our eyes out when his dad and the other deacons finally came out of the doors. Soaked, combed hair. Fancy bathrobes. They looked—it's hard to really say how they looked—content. But, content like a group of siblings who just buried their long-suffering mother who'd been in immense pain the last years of her life and they know she's now at rest. They looked like they'd seen the face of God.

So, we kept following them every Saturday night. We crunched along the gravel just outside the walls, listening to the inside. We were able to figure they weren't using the gym showers, based on the silence in that area of the warehouse. But we followed the wall all the way to the back corner where the clown shower would be, and sure as Armageddon itself we could hear them in there. Beating their chests. Singing hymns, calling for the water to run hotter. Having their sins burned away. Beating and beating their chests until you could hear the deacons crying from their own pain. You'd think they were weeping at the site of a painted saint's icon or John the Baptist's finger bone wrapped in gold foil or something. It makes you wonder what it sounds like when God himself begins to unravel.

Have you ever rinsed off in the clown shower?

I've never used it. But, I was the plumber they would call whenever water wouldn't spray out of his mouth. Happened more than you'd think. I'd arrive after hours and—you can see how short I am—I couldn't reach the mouth on my own. So, I'd walk up to the clown and—you know, he has these big honking purple shoes—so I'd stand on the shoes so I could reach all the way up into the clown's mouth. And the shower head was a lot further back than you'd expect. And, I don't want to sound like a total degenerate of the mind, but I swear it's like the shower head went further and further back into his mouth with each visit. By the end of my contract with the city, I was reaching my entire arm into his mouth just to get a hold of the shower head.

You ever seen a cow give birth? Cause when the calf gets tangled up or whatever, the farm hand has to dive their arm all the way into the cow's womb so the calf can make it out. Grab it by the hooves until they pull it into daylight.

That was me, arm-deep in the mouth. And when the water finally broke free—I admit it—I'd stay there in the shower for a bit.

Have you ever rinsed off in the clown shower?

Of course, it's where I was baptized. Hell, I even lost my first tooth there. The drain swallowed it right up.

"TO WITNESS"

Soon Jones

Hours before sunrise on the first new moon of the year, Cameron Park was dragged out of her warm bed by her roommate and best friend Ash to drive down a random dirt road deep in the country, to an old cemetery hidden among the pine trees. There were already other cars there, flashlights disappearing down a deer trail. Ahead of them were small groups of teens, college students, and middle-aged men and women talking softly amongst themselves. Cameron crossed her arms, too tired and annoyed to care about the coyotes howling from the shadows.

"I need to pee," Cameron said.

"You should've gone before we left," Ash said.

"I *did* go. We've been in the car for an hour."

Ash sighed and rolled her eyes.

"We'll leave right after, okay? The tape is only a few minutes long."

"We drove all the way out here for that?"

"Trust me," Ash said.

The abandoned house sat alone in a clearing, two stories with a wraparound porch and falling apart, paint peeling off bleached, rotted wood in long ribbons, giant holes in the roof. Weeds poked through the broken porch steps and kudzu vines grew up the sides, threatening to swallow the house whole.

There were electric lights in the windows. Cameron listened for the rumble of a portable generator as they went inside, but there was only the sound of floorboards creaking and bending under her feet. Graffiti plastered the walls. What furniture remained was draped with a thick layer of dust and cigarette butts. Fast food wrappers, convenience store slushie cups and condoms littered the floor. The house smelled stale and moldy. People gathered in the living room, trash shoved aside so they could sit around an old CRT television with a VCR on top.

The lights flickered, and conversations died mid-sentence. The digits on the VCR's clock rapidly changed, then flashed 4:44 a.m.

The lights went out. The TV turned on.

A lone streetlight in a foggy night, nothing else in sight, not even the ground, in total silence. The tape cut to someone's office. An empty elevator descended with the doors still wide open, a woman cut vegetables in the kitchen as a shadow loomed over her shoulder, a TV displaying a TV displaying a TV into infinity. A different woman with long black hair tied up in a messy bun sat at a desk, staring into the camera, heavy bags under her eyes. The woman spoke, lips moving, but it was all muffled. She scrubbed her face with her hands and leaned back in her chair, staring at the ceiling.

The woman reached down, opened a drawer, and her hand came back up with a sleek black pistol. She leaned forward and stared into the camera, at Cameron. The woman pushed the barrel against her temple as the door opened behind her, and a thick shadow like a physical presence entered the room.

The woman pulled the trigger.

Cameron jumped, but there was no sound. No blood. The screen went black at the very frame before the hammer hit the firing pin, and there was only darkness. Shadows swallowed the room except for the flashing 4:44. Cameron leaned forward, straining to see. The TV was too dark, darker than it would be if it was off. It was like looking into a black hole.

Slowly, the corners filled in with little triangles of muted yellow. The triangles grew larger, eating more of the screen.

Flash of white. A blinking eye. A pure, impossibly black eye.

The TV and the VCR both shut off and the lights didn't come back on. The others turned on their flashlights and cell phones. No one spoke until they were outside, and then either burst into nervous giggles or swearing. Cameron listened as she tried to understand why everyone was so freaked out over what was clearly some film student's class project. She was about to tell Ash to let her sleep next time, and then a guy in a beat-up trucker cap said:

"Dude, that eye has *never* been there before."

"I've been coming to this for like, a year. It always ends when she pulls the trigger," a girl said.

"You know it's fake, right? The presentation with the house is great, but I've seen scarier online," Cameron said loudly.

A few of the others turned and stared at her.

"It's not fake. It's cursed," one girl said.

"How do you know that?" Cameron asked.

"Because my brother was one of the first victims," she said, then walked away with her group, a few of whom gave Cameron the stink-eye.

"What's her problem?" Cameron asked, keeping her voice low.

Ash waited until the others were out of earshot, then smacked Cameron's arm.

"That's Morgan. Her brother disappeared a few years ago, and so did a bunch of his friends. They were one of the first ones to find the house," Ash whispered.

"I mean, that sucks, but no one's disappearing over a tape. Something else happened to them," Cameron said.

"I'm just telling you what I heard," Ash said, shrugging.

#

Cameron couldn't stop thinking about the tape, counting down the days in the lunar cycle. On the next new moon, she was the one who woke Ash at three in the morning, dressed in long jeans and hiking boots with a maglite and an empty bladder.

The showing was the same as before, only with a few new faces in the crowd. The lights flickered, the VCR flashed 4:44, the tape played, and the power was cut after the eye. The others got up to leave, but Cameron ran upstairs.

"Cam! Get back down here!" Ash hissed after her.

Cameron avoided the holes in the floor and searched all the rooms, looking for a generator or someone, anyone, but there was only more trash and decay. She kicked over a pile of crumpled newspapers in an empty room, and a fat palmetto bug scurried out.

"What do you think you're doing?"

Cameron screamed and spun around. It was Morgan, raising her phone up to light her way.

"Look, I'm sorry about your brother. But I want to know who's really behind this," Cameron said.

"I've already searched the house. Every room, every closet. I come early, like daylight early, and wait for someone to show up and plug everything in. But there's no one," Morgan said.

Grown adults scared of a little tape. For some reason it made Cameron angry. She'd drag them all into the twenty-first century by their ears if she had to.

Cameron stormed downstairs and tried to eject the tape, but it wouldn't budge. So she grabbed the entire unplugged VCR. She rolled her eyes: of course it was unplugged. One of the watchers must've pulled the cord after the viewing to keep the myth alive.

"What do you think you're doing?" Morgan demanded, hot on her heels.

"Yeah, Cam, I don't think that's a good idea. Like that's a really, really bad idea, actually," Ash called from the porch, peering in.

"If it's all *real*, then something will play on that TV next new moon. If nothing happens, everyone will know it's fake," Cam said.

"Why do you care so much? Even if it is fake, let people have their fun. Who does it hurt?" Ash asked.

"It hurts a lot of people," Morgan said quietly.

#

The following weekend, Ash went with her friends to the big city while Cameron stayed behind so she could set up an old CRT she had picked up at a thrift store. The VCR she'd stolen sat on top, and she was about to test that she'd plugged the cables in the right place when Morgan arrived.

"I brought snacks," Morgan said, lifting her backpack when Cameron opened the door.

They sat on the floor in the living room and Cameron pressed play. The VCR flashed 4:44 a.m., even though it was only two in the afternoon. She sat beside Morgan and tore into a bag of hot chips as the tape played.

When they reached the end with the eye, the TV didn't shut off and the power stayed on. Cameron smirked, turned to Morgan to tell her this proved someone was messing with the power at the house in the woods.

Then the tape kept playing.

A little boy with dark brown hair and big eyes played in a pile of oak leaves. An old car drove by in the cul-de-sac.

"Can you tell me again what you saw?" a woman asked.

"The boogeyman," he said simply, kicking up leaves.

"What did the boogeyman look like?" the woman asked.

The boy's shadow turned pitch-black, shot up from the ground and bent down over him. The woman screamed and dropped the camera, her shoes running by on screen.

It cut to the same shot of the streetlight from the beginning of the tape and lingered there for a long time. If it wasn't for the swirling fog and the sound of breathing, Cameron would have thought the tape had frozen.

The streetlight flickered, then went out. Something moved in the darkness, coming closer.

"Give me back my son!"

Cameron and Morgan both screamed and grabbed each other. It was the woman again, her voice so loud and crisp it was like she was in the room.

The tape jumped, and the woman stood in a bathroom in her bra and jeans, staring at her reflection in the mirror. The tub was full to the brim with liquid shadow. In the woman's hand was a pair of pliers. She opened her jaw wide, reached in with the pliers, wiggled them back and forth, then with a grimace, yanked out a molar. Another. And another. And another.

The woman spat blood into the sink, and then she cocked her head back and laughed like it was the funniest damn thing she had ever seen. The shadow overflowed from the tub, spreading until it swallowed everything whole.

Cameron sat in the glow of the static, breath held, listening.

After several minutes, Morgan got up and rewound the tape, staring unblinking at the screen as the footage played in reverse, until the little boy sprang from the shadow into light, playing in the leaves again. There Morgan paused, scrubbed forward a few frames, a couple back.

"Look! You see that?" Morgan asked. She tapped a street sign at the edge of the cul-de-sac. Cameron crawled up and focused hard on the sign.

"I can't read it. Let it play."

Morgan rewound and replayed the last few seconds over and over again. Cameron grabbed a pen and wrote down possibilities as she tried to decipher the undefined letters.

"You got it?" Morgan asked.

"Carmichael Circle and Kerrigan Street." Cameron said.

She shared a look with Morgan, both of them weighing whether it was worth the truth.

Morgan swallowed thickly.

"Let's go find it," she said.

#

The further Cam drove into the country, the faster the temperature dropped. Morgan had brought a thin jacket, and Cameron wished she had done the same. The welcome sign of *Emmons, Florida, Home to Nearly Five Thousand Residents*, had frost spidering up the green aluminum.

Pine trees towered on either side, the road littered with so many bright orange needles that the car occasionally slid. Even though it was midwinter, Emmons was vibrant as spring while the rest of Northwest Florida was still brown and yellow.

All of the businesses on Main Street had boarded up doors and broken windows, their hollow insides bursting with tall weeds and flora. Kudzu creeped over the walls and roofs, fire hydrants and roadside parked cars. Posters of missing people were stapled to every inch of the wooden utility poles, taped to what windows remained intact. Shreds of paper fluttered in the wind like dogwood blossoms.

Every hair on the back of Cameron's neck and arms stood straight. Dread shot from the crown of her skull to the soles of her feet, the same sense of dread she sometimes felt walking alone to her car at night.

The neighborhoods branching off the sole commercial street were in worse shape. Entire houses had been swallowed by kudzu, collapsing under their weight. Kerrigan Street was worse than the others. Weeds had pushed up and broken the asphalt into uneven chunks, tree roots tearing through concrete. There were no people, no signs of human life.

Carmichael Circle was overrun with kudzu. Only one house was untouched: 4144. Everything else was in a state of decay, but 4144 looked like it had a fresh coat of white paint. Two stories with a wraparound porch. Cameron leaned over her steering wheel as she drove up, trying to peer through the curtains. It looked like a nicer version of the house in the woods.

"Oh my god, this is it, Cam. This is the yard from the tape," Morgan said, and before Cameron could stop her, she was out of the car and running up the driveway.

Cameron cursed under her breath and parked, grabbed her keys, then chased after Morgan.

"Hey! What do you think you're doing?" Cameron called.

Morgan ignored her. She bounded up the porch steps, turned the handle, and walked right in the front door. By the time Cameron made it inside Morgan was already gone, her boots thudding on the staircase.

There were shoes by the door, some with crusted mud on the bottom. There was no dust on the furniture. It was a normal house, lived in, warm, like the family had only stepped out and would be returning any moment. The layout, though, was the same as the house in the woods, the rooms divided the same way, the walls covered in the same wood paneling, clean and free of graffiti.

Cameron wandered through the first floor. Clean dishes sat in a rack by the sink. Hand towels were draped over the oven door handle and the back of a chair. The refrigerator was completely empty: no food, no ice, no frost, not even shelves. No pictures pinned to the door with magnets, no grocery lists, no family Christmas cards or child's drawings. There were no pictures *anywhere*. Not a single photo frame. Not one portrait.

"*Cam!*" Morgan screamed.

Cameron ran upstairs and found Morgan in the hall, staring inside an open door.

The first thing that drew Cameron's eyes was the wall covered in family photos, a child's scribbled drawings, a collection of missing posters with last known addresses circled in red. Dozens of polaroids were pinned among the posters, most of them self-portraits of the woman from the tape, the flash washing out her skin and creating dark shadows behind her. Some were of the boy, sleeping, others of a woman who must have been her wife, laughing at first, then annoyed, then shouting and reaching out towards the lens while dark shadows loomed in the spaces behind her.

The woman from the tape sat at a desk under the pictures, her head resting on her left arm like she was only sleeping. Half of the desk was clean. The other half was covered in gore spilling out of the other side of the woman's head, bright red and wet, a gun by her right hand. A camcorder on a stack of books pointed at the woman's blank face, her open eyes. Perfectly preserved, like it had all just happened.

Adrenaline slammed into Cameron's bloodstream. She grabbed Morgan and yanked her out of the room, legs shaking, heart in her throat.

"We're going! Right now!" she said.

Morgan jerked her arm free and glared at Cameron.

"We finally find something real, and you want to leave? Don't you know what this means?"

"Yeah, it means I'm going home. I'm returning the tape and the VCR to that house in the woods, and I'm never thinking about any of this ever again," Cameron said.

"If you want to go, go. I'm not stopping you. But I have to find out what happened to my brother," Morgan said, lifting her chin.

The office door opened wider on its own, and a shadowy hand gripped the siding.

Cameron grabbed Morgan's hand again and didn't let go, dragging her down the stairs and out onto the porch. They had only been in the house for minutes, yet suddenly it was full night, no moon in the sky. Only stars.

"Let go of me!" Morgan snapped.

"Behind us!" Cameron cried.

Morgan must have looked, because she stopped fighting and started running, interlocked her fingers with Cameron's as they raced to her kudzu-covered car. They grabbed fistfuls and yanked the vines off the doors and windows and jumped in. The shadow slinked down the porch steps, a pure white face with no nose or mouth, only two impossibly dark eyes.

Cameron turned the key in the starter, and the engine sputtered and went out. She turned the key again, but the engine refused to turn over. Morgan screamed at her to hurry. Cameron stared at the shadow as she carefully turned the key again, held it until the engine caught and rolled over, roared to life.

She threw the car in reverse and peeled out on the kudzu until the tires got enough traction, and then sped away. In the rearview, the shadow stepped out into the street and watched them go.

All the streetlights were on, but there were no lights inside the homes, the churches, not a single neon in the window of any of the businesses. Shadows rippled in the periphery, and one by one, white faces appeared in the darkness, turning as they drove by.

"Cam, look," Morgan said, holding out her phone.

Cameron glanced down at the lock screen, confused. April 4th, 4:44 a.m.

"What? It's the beginning of February," Cameron said, fishing in her pocket for her own phone.

It had the same time. There was no signal, not even a single bar, only ROAMING displayed in the upper corner.

"That's fine," Cameron said, dropping her phone in the drink holder. "I'll get a new phone tomorrow; everything will be okay then."

They passed the town sign, exiting Emmons, and only then did Cameron sigh and sink back against her seat, relaxing as they drove through the corridor of pine trees. Heavy fog crept in, erasing the stars above and the trees on the sides of the road, until Cameron couldn't see the road past the front of her hood.

A single streetlight shone in the distance, inching closer as miles spun beneath them. The headlights failed, and the road disappeared completely. Morgan held her hand and squeezed. Cameron accelerated until she was racing towards the streetlight, shadows pressed against the windows.

#

On the night of a new moon, groups of strangers once more congregated to an abandoned house in the middle of the woods, dim fluorescent lights calling them closer. College students passed bottles of liquor and beer among themselves, jumping at the distant howls of coyotes.

Inside the house, an old VCR flashed 4:44.

The lights went out.

The television came on.

"DAS WEIBCHEN JEDER TIERART"

Laura Keating

Is this thing working? [*thudthudthud*] I see the tape moving, the wheels turning. Doesn't matter, I guess. Probably no one will find it, won't listen for years, if ever. Just there's a part of me that feels like it's something I should do, before I forget. [*Clears throat*]

This is what happened to me after my landlord died.

Five weeks ago, he dropped dead on his way home one night from the dépanneur, the one up on rue St-Viateur—like the bagels. Some kids saw him clutch his chest as his heart gave one last, thunderous clap and that was it, he was dead by the time they got to him. I saw the police cars pull up to our brownstone at the top of rue Waverly that night. Mrs. Kocher, his widow, told me the next morning.

"Are you going to be okay?" I asked. I was on my way to work, had my Ubisoft messenger bag slung over one shoulder. She didn't look up, crouched in her tiny front garden and pulling out weeds with her delicate hands. They shook badly; she looked cold in the spring air, even bundled up.

She said, "I'll manage."

I thought about it all day, this poor old lady alone. After work, I bought her a card from the pharmacy on Ave. du Parc. Wholly inadequate, but at least I was trying, I thought. As a last-minute bit of generosity, I wrote under my name: *Let me know if there is anything I can do to help.*

She called the next day. She could have come upstairs—I was home—and she knew that, but she'd never been in my apartment. She has propriety like that. Doesn't like to go into a young man's place alone. Whenever I had a leaky faucet or broken heater, it was Mr. Kocher who'd come up. And fast, too. He was a great handyman. Never said a word— he couldn't. Mrs. Kocher explained when I'd signed my lease, holding my breath for dear life in their cramped kitchen, that he'd survived mouth cancer in the early '90s but it had claimed his tongue.

Why hold my breath? Well, between you and me, the stink was unbearable. Unknowably powerful. I know now but…well, let me get to that.

I don't think he bathed much, Mr. Kocher. Once he came to my apartment to fix my broken back door, and he had to stay squatted in my kitchenette for over an hour as he replaced the hardware. "Pungent" doesn't even begin to describe it. Like raw onions, or Irish stew mixed with an old man funk, like greasy hair and dust. A stink to burn the hair out of your nostrils. I had to hide in my home office, windows flung open to the Montreal winter to escape. When he left, I had to air the whole place out and burn incense. The Kocher apartment smelled constantly like that, but worse: warm and trapped, a miasma of bad cooking and body odor. It was so strong it would seep up through the warped cracks in my old wood floor, would eek out from loose corners in my closet. I had to buy a separate, zippered standing closet for my suits and buttoned shirts because the smell would get into my clothes. I swear to God, into my clothes! The Kochers aired their home out exactly once every year, the first warm day after winter. If I had my windows open at the same time, the smell would roll in from outside. At least after that it was marginally better for a few weeks. I make good money as a videogame producer, could move somewhere else, but I love this location. Mile End is cool. It wasn't always, it was considered a slum back in the mid-1940s when the Kocher family bought this place, probably for a pot of potatoes and a song. Place is worth a million now. Mr. Kocher grew up here, moved out at eighteen, and started renting the top floor out in the early '80s, when he'd inherited it, and he and his wife moved in downstairs. My rent—and it's cheap, I'll tell you that much—is their main source of income. Or it was.

But about that phone call.

I listened to Mrs. Kocher carefully; her landline connection was loose, the air on the phone full of static.

"I don't know what to do with everything," she told me. "Hermann had so much stuff, so many papers, and I just need some help bagging it up, getting rid of a couple things."

I was regretting the card but told her I'd take a look.

The door was open when I went downstairs. I knocked on the frame as I let myself in, calling, "Hello? Mrs. Kocher?"

She called back from the kitchen. "Come on in, you can keep your shoes on."

I noticed immediately that the smell wasn't as strong. Still present, had probably soaked into curtains and carpets, but not as heady. She popped her head around the corner of the hallway and beckoned me inside, smiling. "I've made lunch; sit down before we get to work."

Mrs. Kocher looks like an old art teacher: long skirts, flowing shawls, wrists adorned with clinking bangles and gaudy rings on her slim fingers. For her age she looks incredible. Strong nose, fine lines around her green eyes. Her rusty hair never fully grayed, and she keeps it up in a messy jaw-clip, little tendrils tumbling loose around her face. The sort of face that you can tell was a smoke-show once.

I sat down at the tiny wooden table. She'd set out a tablecloth laid with bowls and plates for us each. I was going to tell her that I'd already eaten, but she seemed so pleased to have someone to have lunch with that I couldn't say no. The soup was a simple broth with sprigs of some vegetable and tiny white meatballs. The bread she served was crusty, and still hot from the oven. When the soup was finished, she piled me a plate of ham, potatoes, and asparagus topped off with a glazed gravy. She apologized for the simple fare. I'm telling you right now—and I can't explain how—it tasted better than almost anything I'd eaten, and I've dined at some world-class restaurants. If Mr. Kocher had eaten like this every day, he'd lived like a king.

And all this time, I'd thought I was smelling bad cooking.

Lunch ended; she poured two short glasses of wine the color of lemonade. A digestif, she explained, that she made herself. Like the meal, it was also fantastic. I sat back with satisfaction, the kind you only get from a perfect lunch.

She knit her fingers together as she asked, "Was everything okay?" She looked apprehensive.

I told her it was amazing, and she looked surprised as well as delighted. She blushed a little, like she didn't often get complimented, and I wondered if Mr. Kocher had, by the end, taken her skills for granted. I spied a picture of the old guy through the wide arch between the kitchen and the living room.

I took my drink with me as I walked to the mantel. On it was an old photograph, black and white. It showed a much younger Mr. Kocher, dressed in white trousers and shirt and sturdy boots one fist on his hip gripping a hard-brimmed hat, feet spread in a wide, imposing stance. The plants and trees around him bore huge, waxy leaves with sharp, scaly stalks.

"That was taken in 1962, just before he discovered me."

Mrs. Kocher had appeared at my shoulder. She was smiling wistfully at her late husband. "He was just twenty-four, and already so well-traveled. He was such a handsome man."

"Discovered?" I asked. She nodded.

"I was his protégée. We were world-famous explorers, didn't you know?"

I whipped my head around. "I had no idea."

"Hermann was a zoologist. I can't tell you how many papers he wrote, how many books."

She moved around the room pointing at various pictures. "There we are, just a month after that other picture was taken."

I had not been wrong; she had been stunning. Dressed the same: floor-length skirt, bangles, long hair—though not clipped up. A child of the '60s if I ever saw one. Mrs. Kocher was continuing her guided tour of the photos. There were hundreds.

Hermann on the top of Kilimanjaro, at the valley near the Bezeklik Thousand Buddha Caves of Turpan, crouched by a sandy pit in the Jiaohe Ruins. There he was in Cambodia: Angkor Wat, Ta Prohm, Bayon in Angkor Thom. Here, looking stern at Loch Ness, on a boat in Bermuda, hiking Bluff Creek in California, the Gobi Desert… They'd been everywhere.

I looked over each picture. "Where are you in all these photos?"

She smiled, but a little sorrowfully. "Behind the camera."

There was only one other photo of her, black and white, smiling on the steps of this very building, holding a small, swaddled bundled in her arms.

"You have kids?"

She nodded. "We had many children. I always wanted more. But finally, Hermann said he was done, he'd had enough." She stared at the old photo in silence, a forlorn weight behind her green eyes.

There was not a single child's photo in the room.

"Where are they now?"

She shook her head. "I haven't seen them in years. Hermann… He never enjoyed being a father."

I looked into the stern, young face of Hermann Kocher. I had always thought he was a pretty nice guy. Seemed to adore his wife, couldn't take his smiling eyes off her whenever I'd seen them together. But what did I know? Mrs. Kocher limped while she walked me around the room. I realized, in the five years I'd lived upstairs, I had never seen her outside except gardening the small patch of front lawn or kissing Mr. Kocher goodbye on the step as he went on one of his long walks. I couldn't tell if this was a new or old injury.

I asked, "Are you okay, Mrs. Kocher?"

She thought a moment. "Please call me Chloé. And I'm simply missing a leg." She smiled impishly. "Bitten off by a crocodile."

My mouth fell open. "You're kidding."

She was laughing again. "I can assure you, I'm not. Would you like to see?"

Without ado, she lifted her skirts and I saw her legs.

"So it was," I agreed. I can't tell you why it didn't seem strange. In fact, I was finding I really liked her spirited personality. I imagined she would have been quite the gal to know in her day.

She limped past me, beckoning with one hand. She led me to the basement stairs. She asked if I could get started down there, she had work to do up here.

I asked, "What do you want me to get rid of?"

She waved her hand. It would all have to go, she said.

The smell I associated with Mr. Kocher got stronger as I went down the stairs. I turned on the light as I reached the bottom.

The paneled basement was carpeted in the finest orange and white shag 1974 had to offer. A grandfather's subterranean den, stuffed with boxes of old files, stacks of newspapers, and binders. The shelves were book mountains. A garbage-covered desk with an ancient computer sat in the corner beside another bookshelf laden with three TVs and one Sony VCR. The space not taken up by assorted media was filled with glass cases of animal parts—taxidermy, I mean: a dusty buck's head with three, wild, staring eyes, a reptilian tail, humungous shark teeth, a petrified monkey paw, pinned butterflies the size of dinner plates. There were none of the pretty little touches Mrs. Kocher—Chloé—had applied upstairs. I ventured further into the basement.

Down a small hallway, I found a dark water closet with a cracked sink and stained toilet. Beyond that was a spartan bedroom, with a sagging wrought-iron bed, splintering wooden chair, and a rusty bucket. A greasy pair of corduroy trousers was draped over the end of the bed; the quilt was deeply stained, the damaged pillow looked like a Civil War bandage. There was a padlock on the inside of the door. The smell was the worst in here. I returned quickly to the main basement.

I started cleaning the desk. Under piles of refuse were old newspaper clippings and once more I was met with the stern, intelligent gaze of the young Hermann Kocher. One tantalizing headline read: "Startling Discovery Mystifies, Divides Scientific Community." However, the subsequent article had been censored with a heavy, black marker. All the clippings were like that. I frowned and flipped though several magazines on the desk. They started out decent (classic National Geographics and Time magazines) but the closer I got to the top of the pile, the more recent publications, the more irreputable they became: *Out There!*, *Uncanny Monthly*, *They're Real!*, and the good old *World Weekly News*. But no matter the journal's pedigree, all the related articles (and sometimes headlines) had been destroyed, leaving only the grim face and keen, dark eyes of Hermann Kocher.

I dropped the ruined magazines to the floor, and a puff like crypt dust rose from their pages. I was wondering if I shouldn't be wearing a mask when something that had been hidden under the magazines caught my eye: a tape recorder.

It's what I'm recording on now, taping over one of the old cassettes. I don't think he would have minded.

Mr. Kocher had hundreds of tapes scattered around his desk, spread out like puzzle pieces amongst balled up old tissues, scribbled notes, moldy coffee cups. I had no idea what to do with anything. I called up the stairs to say that I needed some garbage bags, and Mrs. Kocher—Chloé, sorry—tossed me down a box. I ballooned one open and began filling it with everything from the desk. For something to do while I worked, I popped in one of the tapes: June 2019.

It was empty. I tried another, September 2016.

The same dead air. Then, I heard a cough. I stopped and listened more closely, turning the volume up. There was breathing, slow and deep, and a chittering sound like old bed springs, and something else…a gentle but swift, impatient clicking (*tick, tick, tick, tick…*) and soft scratching, like nails on wood. I hit fast forward. Nearly the whole tape was like that (the clicking and scratching was gone before the end). I found another and popped it inside. It was the same. I turned up the volume, tried older dates: 1999, '97, '94. There were nearly 400 tapes, one a month all the way back to June 1992. All the same steady breathing, the chittering, and that *clicking…*

"I NEED TO KNOW."

I leapt back from the deep voice, and then snatched the volume dial, turning it back down. There were hurried footsteps on the floorboards overhead.

"Everything alright?" Chloé called.

"Fine," I shouted back. When she was gone, I kept listening. Although I had never heard him speak, I knew this rich, finely accented voice belonged to Mr. Kocher.

"*…think this will end it. They cannot survive if they cannot get out.*" There came a small sob. I realized with some alarm that the man on the tape was crying. "*I'm sorry, my darling. So sorry.*"

His breathing quickened, there was a choking gasp, then a whimpering moan, rising to a scream. The screaming didn't stop but became horrified, confused, and then muffled, like he'd gagged his own mouth. There came a second voice on the tape, her tone unmistakable, terrified and concerned. Approaching footsteps and then Mrs. Kocher's own screams joined her husband's horror and dismay.

"*N-nein, nein! Was hast du getan! Schatz, was hast du getan!*"

The recording stopped abruptly. The tape kept playing, but it was dead air.

I stopped the tape.

I can't tell you why I didn't leave, why I didn't tie up the bag of trash, go back upstairs, and say I was done. Maybe even then I knew it was too late. Sometimes something gets into you, and you must know, must see it through.

I felt no need to call Chloé downstairs, have her explain and relive whatever happened that day. No need to upset an old lady. I kept filling the bags, the voice from the tape echoing in my head. Chloé came downstairs soon with another drink for me, and to ask how I was getting on. By the dim light of the basement, the fine lines around her eyes seemed to vanish and her hair appeared darker, and once again I was struck by how beautiful she would have once been. She placed a hand on my shoulder as she thanked me, and a not unwelcome shiver ran down my back. I offered to help her up the stairs, but she laughed, a pretty little sound, and assured me she could manage.

I got back to work.

With the magazines and newspapers from on and around the desk trashed, the room was already appearing saner. I started on the bookshelves, reading out the titles on the spines:

Beyond the Last Mountain; Uncovering the Wildman; Lesser-Known Creatures of the Peruvian Deserts, and their Habits; Cryptozoological Principles and Field Work; The Notion of a Trap.

At least forty of the books were written by Mr. Kocher himself. I noted the standby light of the VCR was on, a tape inside. The TV screen crackled with dust and a low, electric whine filled the room as I turned it and the tape player on. I hit play.

The video buzzed to life.

Mr. Kocher as I knew him, bearded, old, and tired, sat in profile at the desk. The desk I'm sitting at now. It was behind me then and, looking around, I saw the video camera on its tripod. He kept his head down as he worked. I leaned closer to the TV, nose nearly to the screen.

He held a black marker, destroying all his old interviews, articles, and research.

I popped the tape out of the VCR. Printed on the label in a fine script was a date. It had been made just three months earlier.

I opened one of the drawers in the bookshelves and found what I had hoped for: a video library. I found the oldest recording, an interview from 1959.

The black and white image was clear, the sound warbling but audible. An older man in a neat suit with narrow lapels reclined in a Bauhaus chair, smoking a cigarette as he talked to a handsome young man seated across from him.

"Und Sie haben diese Tiere geshen?" Their voices sounded like they were coming from the bottom of a well.

"Oh, ja. Gelegentlich," replied the young Mr. Kocher. *"Aber die wahren Erkentnisse erlangt man auf der Jagd, nicht bei dem Fund."*

"Wie meinen Sie das?"

The young Hermann Kocher thought a moment. Briefly, he switched to English. *"Well, given the nature of the work, you must understand, I come across many frauds or fairy tales."* Both men laughed. *"Aber in solchen Fällen wird meine Forschung sozialwissenschaftlich anstatt zoologisch."*

"Der Mensch ist auch eben ein Tier."

"Genau."

Not to be unmatched, the interviewer also tried out his English skills. It occurred to me they must have been broadcasting from near a military base, where both languages were common.

"And what has been your most dangerous encounter?"

Hermann laughed and flashed a charming smile. *"Na, in allen Fällen ist das Weibchen jeder Tierart tödlicher als das Männchen."*

I turned off the tape.

I want to say that I didn't know what I was looking for. I want to say that.

But I can't.

I watched several more tapes and found what I was not looking for in 1965. Chloé appeared on film. I felt my stomach twist as she floated down the side of a lush Scottish hill, long dress billowing, beckoning the cameraman on with a smile and wave of her hand.

In 1971, Hermann and Chloé together held up the body of a hairless, doglike creature with bulbous eyes (fogged in death) and a spiny ridge along its back. A crew joined them then, the footage cut with newsreel.

In 1975, a large, hair-covered beast ran from the couple in a dark, piney woods.

In 1982, Chloé was crying, her eyes streaming, pleading at the camera, while babies bawled and shrieked from the adjoining room. The living room upstairs. Hermann, unseen, held the video camera.

Chloé begged, *"Please, put it away, put that damn thing away! You know I don't understand—"*

"I won't do it! I won't have another one of those little monsters!"

"Hermann, please. Please don't say that. Stop."

"Davor bringe ich mich um, verstehst du? I've had enough!"

"Don't say—"

"This has to stop. I want it to stop. I want it to—" He choked. Chloé's pleading eyes turned to worry and fear.

"Darling, it will be alright. Please lie down."

He coughed. *"I'm…sorry."*

"I know."

"I love you."

"I know."

I stopped the tape. There was only one more: May 1992. Written below the date, in the same elegant script, one word: *Birth.*

I started the tape.

Hermann sat alone in this basement. Not as old as I knew him, but no longer young. He was withered, exhausted, as he looked directly into the camera. The handsome young man was gone. He swallowed hard as he closed his eyes and stuck a finger into the side of his mouth.

"Not long," he said, hoarsely. "Recording before I forget. They say you forget the pain of birth, it's true." He glanced over his shoulders, to the stairs. "This will be the last."

He began to gag. His head tipped back, his throat bulged, tears streamed from his eyes as he gripped the desk, shaking. I couldn't look away.

His stifled whimpers filled the room. Something long and delicate rose from his mouth, black and bristled, wrapped around the side of his cheeks, climbed…

The tape finished.

I was not surprised to see Chloé in the black glass of the TV screen, standing behind me. I turned.

The flesh of her forehead had become papery, her eyes waxen. A word crossed my mind: *Molting.*

It's how many species rejuvenate.

She was no longer wearing her skirts, but I'd already seen what was beneath them upstairs. I guess that was the test. She really had lost a leg – but she has several more to spare. She didn't have to ask if I was afraid, she knew the answer, just as I knew that it had not been a digestif. Some species use pheromones to attract a partner; others evolve different skills.

That was five weeks ago.

She had Hermann destroy his papers, but she's never understood things like tape recorders. She's very old. It's an adorable little quirk of my Chloé's.

Before I forget, I'll leave this tape here.

There is a strong taste on my tongue, which has new little ridges in the back, grips, rising from my abdomen, which is no longer flat. My sweat has changed, too: heady, no matter how much I bathe. It'll be soon. Work was confused when I gave my notice, but Chloé says it's time to get out of the city. The sale of this old brownstone will set us up for decades. She and Hermann had a small cabin up north, a cozy, secluded place and enough space to grow. She's going to take me there. I'm so excited.

We're going to start a family.

"EMILY BUYS LOT 1806: A 19TH CENTURY PHOTO ALBUM WITH INSCRIPTION, ALTHOUGH SHE DOESN'T MEAN TO"

Elou Carroll

She is at the auction house to buy one lot and one lot only. She has the company card and strict orders. Emily has always been good at following orders; she is the hotel's best staff member, or so her manager always says.

Emily is at the auction house to buy one lot and one lot only.

And yet—

#

DESCRIPTION IN BRIEF
Leather-bound with intricate debossed foil design. Foil hot-stamped with genuine gold, some flaking in places. Interior pages crafted from thick card stock

with some water damage—other damages catalogued to follow—and separated with thin tissue. Frames are die-cut in various styles, fashionable in the era, with gold foil detailing. Lot 1806 is made complete with a set of twenty photographs, referred hereafter as Plates, whose captions are written in faded pencil.

INSCRIPTION
Written in jagged pencil—the fatal stab of the full-stop has dented the card stock and the image beneath. It reads

Evelyn,
So you remember.

\#

She hadn't meant to raise her paddle—bidding number 392—but something about it calls to her without her notice. It creeps on her shoulder and claws up her neck and whispers, Buy me, Emily. Take me home.

Emily is at the auction to buy tables, little nesting tables with velvet on the top, for the hotel in which she works. Something to add a little character to the hallways. Maybe, they'll put vases on them with fake flowers. Flowers that cannot die.

Emily hadn't meant to bid on the photo album.
And yet—

\#

PLATE I

A small tear splits the top right corner of the
protective tissue, and there is discoloration in the
center—a ghost of the image below is present
though, curiously, the eyes in the photograph are
closed while the tissue bears open eyes, wide,
afeared.

The frame is a modest oval, ringed with a thin
thread of gold. Captioned simply Eudora in that
same pointed script.

Eudora sits simply with her hands in her lap,
chin raised high. Even with her eyes closed, she is
striking. High cheekbones, eyebrows arched like the
pointed frames of church doorways. She could be in
a church, there are faint shadows across her face
which could be the distorted pattern of a stained
glass window. We have been unable to verify the
exact location, nor the photographer, but there is a
cast across her countenance, a set in her shoulders
that seems holy.

PLATE II

A curious image takes the second place in the
album—an overcast landscape set in a rectangular
frame, ornate golden foil in arabesques around it
with but a small space left unblemished for the
caption. The page itself carries brown spots of age, as
if it might be older still than the rest of the album.

A blackening blooms from the pit of the spine, spreading across the page in sickly gray. It is hard to discern the origin of the mold-like stain, and our valuers have purported that it could have been intentional.

Protective tissue is creased but otherwise undamaged.

Turning our attention back to the photograph: nestled in rolling hills, growing out of a sheer, stone cliff like a mushroom, is a sprawling manor across five storys. It is difficult to see the state of the manor from this distance but the photographer has employed soft focus to draw the eye to its lofty awnings. It is not our opinion that PLATE I was taken in the same locale. However, we do wonder at the connection between the two.
Another brief caption follows. *Hallowhall, at a distance.*

#

She hadn't meant to go to the house—not that it was there anymore—but she's parked her car on the gravel regardless. The photo album sits on the passenger seat. Emily doesn't remember opening it, but Hallowhall stares back at her from the grubby upholstery. Hallowhall as it was. It would have made a wonderful hotel in its day.

Emily steps out of the car and sees the house in the space where it isn't. Such a shame, Emily, *says a voice.* Such a shame.

Emily traces the photo with a finger, the photo album a comforting weight in her arms. Perhaps there's something she can use here. Perhaps the hotel could be better, could be grander, just like Hallowhall when it was a house still standing.

Emily hadn't meant to go to the house.

And yet—

#

PLATE III

Eudora returns to the frame in PLATE III. A circle is cut in the center of the card stock, with another simple foil adornment.

Eudora, close but not… Closed, reads that same sharp pencil above. The back of the photograph features words in a different script—*Unusable scrap. All of them, worthless!* Someone, however, must have deemed this particular photograph worthy of inclusion.

It is out of focus.

Eudora's arms are outstretched and she appears to be dancing. We cannot discern any facial expression or clothing details, beyond that they are light—translucent. The sunlight and the lack of focus make Eudora look like she is glowing.

PLATE IV

Another curious ghost shadows across the protective tissue on PLATE IV. Not one figure, but many. A faceless crowd. Perhaps, just finger smudges. Perhaps, something else. Whatever they are, they certainly have not been pressed on the tissue from the image beneath.

Particularly decorative, the frame on PLATE IV is ornate in its shape. Curves and corners both, it bestows upon the enframed image an air of importance.

It is here that we are introduced to the once-owner of this peculiar collection. *Evelyn and Eudora,* announces the scratchy caption. The familiar Eudora has her eyes cast modestly toward the bottom of the frame but Evelyn challenges the camera—gaze squared directly at the center of the lens. Her eyes burn with something—defiance, perhaps. She looks like her sister but sharper, as if she has been taken across a whetstone, her edges buffed to lethal points. Evelyn does not smile. Evelyn holds her sister's shoulder with a fierceness that pales her knuckles and creases Eudora's dress. If Eudora feels any pain, it does not show in her face.

Behind Eudora, there is a shadow.

The more we look at it, the darker it becomes.

#

She doesn't mean to avoid mirrors — well, she does, but she doesn't want to. Emily doesn't want to avert her eyes whenever she passes the mirrors in the hallways, in the suites, in the foyer. It's ridiculous, really. Silly nonsense that she should have grown out of by now. Emily was always a fearful girl; there were always monsters under the bed, in the wardrobe, outside of her window.

Now, there is a shadow in the mirror. When she passes, the shadow follows after. It never steps out from the glass, but Emily feels it behind her still, even when she's in the linen closet, surrounded by nothing but bedding and towels and fresh, clean smells.

Emily doesn't mean to avoid mirrors.

And yet —

#

PLATE V

Eudora laughs in PLATE V, captioned simply *Before*. The image itself is creased, as if it has been folded and then straightened back out.

In its entirety, PLATE V is simple — there is no foiling, the card stock is blank but for that single scribble, and the frame itself is just a rectangle. Eudora, too, is dressed simply in a straight, white nightgown with her hair resting long over her shoulders.

Due to the nature of photography in the early 19th century, the photograph is not perfectly sharp.

There are echoes of Eudora at her edges, each of them laughing as she does. It looks to have been taken and developed with devotion—and then ruined later by a different hand.

PLATE VI

Lot 1806 now brings us back to Hallowhall—closer this time. *Evelyn, Eudora and* [the third name has been erased] *at the Entrance to Hallowhall.* A large door stands shut behind them, ivy creeping across it.

Evelyn stands with her arms crossed, but something akin to a smile teases at the corners of her mouth.

Eudora, too, is amused, holding a finger in front of her lips as if to conceal a secret. This sister grins and holds her skirts out to the side with her other hand. They stand together as co-conspirators. Twin flames on wilted candles. Crumpled buds waiting to bloom.

The figure next to them is male but his identity is indiscernible. Someone—perhaps Evelyn, perhaps the captions' mysterious author—has taken a pin or some such to the photograph and scratched away his face, damaging the card stock to the side with their vigor. Whatever face there might have been is completely irreparable now.

#

Emily doesn't know why she's standing outside of the hotel—still, waiting—but she stands there anyway, even with the rain soaking her clothes and pooling at her feet. She looks up at the sky and a laugh rushes up from her chest.

She hasn't laughed like this in days. The hotel is struggling and the manager is away, and there is only Emily left to fix it. Only Emily to mop the floors and clean the rooms. Only Emily to check guests in and check them out again. Emily hasn't been home in—she's not quite sure. It's not a large place, the hotel, only five rooms and a small breakfast, lunch and dinner service. The chef is inside and Emily should probably go inside too. There will be meals waiting for their tables—scant though they are.

Funny, isn't it? *says the voice, and Emily replies,* Yes. I don't know why, but yes.

Emily doesn't know why she's standing outside of the hotel, soaking in the rain.

And yet—

#

PLATE VII

PLATE VII is taken just as Eudora enters Hallowhall. She casts a glance over her shoulder but her eyes do not meet the lens. Instead, they fix upon a blurred figure at the edge of the photograph. The figure is Evelyn—there is no caption to tell us so but we know. We know.

There are scratches in the card stock. If we tilt the photo album just so, we can make out a faint impression of the word *Don't*.

PLATE VIII

The door is closed now and Evelyn is baring her teeth—her smile as wide and bright as a furnace burning. Her hand is clasped in the unknown figure's, his fingers digging deep into her skin. His face scratched out.

As with PLATE II, the card stock here too is decorated with blooming black spores like mushrooms pressed flat.

The caption reads, *This is the moment. This is the thing that you cannot take back.*

\#

She doesn't remember coming back inside and closing the door—but there it is, closed, behind her. She doesn't try to open it; the shiver in her neck tells her it wouldn't open anyway.

Shrewd, *says a voice.* Very shrewd.
She tries not to think about the door. If she doesn't think about it, it is just a door, a door that is just closed. She wets her lips and makes her way to the kitchen.

Emily doesn't remember coming back inside and closing the door.

And yet—

\#

PLATE IX

A new hand writes the caption for PLATE IX; it is shaky, as if the penman were infirm at the time of writing. The letters are muddled, but their message is clear: *I didn't mean it. I swear, I didn't mean it.*

Both protective tissue and card stock are near completely black—the only respite is the small well in which the remorseful pencil rests. It is cold to the touch.

Hallowhall peers oppressive from the frame with Eudora in one window, hands pressed white against the cracked glass. Behind her there is the shadow. Always the shadow. The black smoke of its hand rests upon her shoulder. Her eyes have been gouged out.

PLATE X

The dents from the gouging in the previous plate have come through onto the protective tissue and photograph both on PLATE X. The force of the pencil stab leaves dimples in Evelyn's cheeks—in this photograph she is laughing, her sister still pounding on the window behind.

The frame is water-damaged, as if by tears. Did Evelyn weep for her sister? We can never know but the caption has been erased; the evidence, shavings of rotten rubber, is caught in the groove of the album's spine. Clinging to its bones like a secret told.

#

She doesn't mean to avoid the windows, but she does now, too. The shadow, once confined in the mirrors, presses its long, dark fingers on the window panes. Emily doesn't look outside anymore, staring instead at the wallpaper, at the doors, at the guests as they move past her, careful not to touch.

You're scaring them, *says the voice.*

I know, *says Emily.* I'm scared too.

Emily doesn't mean to avoid the windows.

And yet —

#

PLATE XI

The door is open. The camera is on its side. The shadow is closer now and Eudora is gone from the window.

Faintly, we can see Evelyn running down the great corridor in Hallowhall's entryway, her figure fading into the dark. In the foreground, a blurred boot turns away.

PLATE XII

There is no photograph on PLATE XII though the remnants of glue linger in the ripped frame. Where the card stock should be clean cream, it is instead covered in overlapping pencil. It is difficult to tell which hand this scrawl belongs to—it could even be my own.

Eudora in the darkness. Eudora all alone. Eudora in the darkness and Evelyn, she is gone. Eudora in the darkness. Eudora all alone. Eudora in the darkness and Evelyn, she is gone. Eudora in the darkness. Eudora all alone. Eudora in the darkness and Evelyn, she is gone. Eudora in the darkness. Eudora all alone. Eudora in the darkness and Evelyn, she is gone. Eudora in the darkness. Eudora not alone. Eudora in the darkness and Evelyn's coming home.

There is a shadow on the page.

#

She doesn't mean to talk in circles when the manager calls from his holiday letting down south, but she can't help it. Emily repeats every third sentence, as if she herself is a poem, a song, a broken record. To his credit, the manager does not comment on her strange new speaking pattern, and Emily pretends it's not happening at all.

She doesn't realize that she's holding the photo album close to her chest. Emily is focusing on her other hand, her finger that coils in the old phone cord, tighter and tighter until it hurts.

Emily doesn't mean to talk in circles.
And yet.

#

PLATE XIII

Lot 1806 changes tack here. Evelyn and Eudora are children, jovial and smiling. The figure behind them, perhaps their mother or a governess, does not smile. She holds them both as if keeping them still, her nails nicking the skin of their throats, though the sisters do not notice—too caught up in each other. In the game.

There is a pattern to the frame like damask wallpaper. The caption, in comparison, is simple.

A Beginning.

PLATE XIV

Ripped from the album, the protective tissue is missing—the caption appears to acknowledge its absence. *Nothing to protect now. All gone, all gone.*

We—*I*—wanted to skip PLATE XIV, wanted to turn you away from it and back to another Lot. It is my duty, however.

PLATE XIV is Eudora in repose. Laid out in her coffin with mourners beside. Evelyn is gaunt in the pews, not standing like her peers but staring just above the open coffin. Her hollow eyes are wide.

Eudora's face is *wrong* somehow. Not that same wrongness that one finds in the process of preserving a body. No. Rather, something is missing. There is something that was in her that has been taken. Devoured.

The shadow is above Eudora. Its mouth—for it has such a dreadful mouth—is open wide.

#

She remembers a winter in the dark, a winter with the power out and all the candles all used up. Emily is a child in this December remembrance and her father has made up a game.

We'll tell stories, *says her father,* and because it's dark, because we can't see to the end of our fingers— Well, who's to say the stories aren't real?

That winter, Emily learns to love the dark.

Emily learns to love the dark.

And yet—

#

PLATE XV

Evelyn is coming home, reads the caption of PLATE XV. The frame appears to cling to the image, as if the card stock has microscopic setules that grasp and pull at the photograph. In fact, the page itself has a strange texture to it—like the paper has been made of pulp by inexperienced hands. If you look closely, the grain calls forth images of pallid spiders preserved and flattened.

I daren't look at the photograph but I must. I must. For who else will catalogue Lot 1806 if not I?

She stares out of the print. Grinning. Mouth contorting. Teeth loose in her gums and her tongue blackened, engorged. Eudora, no longer pretty as she ought to be but flushed with a euphoria only achievable by those who do not need to fear death any longer.

The shadow is in her eyes.

PLATE XVI

Evelyn is coming home, says that same shaky hand from plates previous. The tissue and card stock are stained with soil and in the photograph Evelyn stands tall with her fists clenched, shoulders set back, in front of Hallowhall.

The house's door is open, beckoning her to enter, but Evelyn stands fast—she does not falter.

#

She hasn't left the hotel in days. The guests are beginning to notice the shadows beneath her eyes, the way she is always looking over her shoulder. Still, they come. It's such a lovely hotel, after all. Close enough to the local amenities without being in the town proper. Just the right amount of countryside for these stuffy city folk.

Where are you going? asks the voice.

Emily doesn't answer.

Emily hasn't left the hotel in days.

And yet—

#

PLATE XVII

But Evelyn will not stay.

She stands, we presume, in front of Hallowhall but the camera is fixed upon her face, bleached lighter than white. Over-exposed save for her eyes which reflect flames upon flames. On her cheek, a burn.

PLATE XVIII

Hallowhall is on fire and the trees around it too are being eaten by the hungry flames. A silhouette—Evelyn, we're certain—is cast coal black against their light. Watching, waiting for Hallowhall to go, Eudora and the shadow with it.

#

She can't tell them why she did it, the manager, the police. Emily can't tell them how she got the canisters or why she had her father's lighter in her pocket. She can't even tell them when it happened.

But she can tell them about the voice, about how it screamed, Nonononononono, in her ear until it hurt. They think she means the guests, the chef stuck in the kitchen, the three people who perished and blackened and charred. They are not listening, not really.

Her hand is on the photo album. They do not seem to notice.

Emily can't tell them why she did it.
And yet—

#

PLATE XIX

The card stock is burned. Great chunks have been charred away but the photograph remains intact. Evelyn is older now, smiling, with a brood of children tucked beneath her arms. Behind her, on the wall, is the faint shape of a person.

PLATE XX

The last photograph is murky but the same as the previous. PLATE XX is underexposed, the same happy family smiling out though they are all blackened as if by soot. The shadow in the background is more prominent here, more fully formed and the words beneath it set my teeth clacking.

Eudora, close.

#

She tries not to look at the shape in the mirror—not a mirror really, but a window she cannot see through. They can see her through it though, whoever is on the other side. They've left her alone, but Emily knows they're watching. They would be silly not to.

There cannot possibly be a shape in the mirror. There cannot be a shape because she got rid of it. The hotel, the shadow, the photo album. All of it.

The photo album is beneath her hand, but Emily doesn't notice.

Emily tries not to look at the shape in the mirror; the shape in the mirror no longer exists, if it ever existed at all. Emily tries not to look at the shape in the mirror.

And yet—

"COOKING_ALONE@NIGHT"

Aristo Couvaras

{*Profile Picture*}
Cooking_Alone@Night 3wks ago [Follow]
     Paravani, Georgia (Music: *A Cookbook for Cannibals* by Binding Prometheus)

A fixed camera points down at a figure standing behind a kitchen island. The countertop is glistening black stone, there is a wooden cutting board and a large Damascus steel knife resting next to it; the overhead light plays on the striations of the blade.

The figure's face cannot be seen. The camera shows only their torso—clad in a plain black hoodie, sleeves rolled up to the elbows, exposing skinny arms. The figure is wearing black nitrile cooking gloves. An object just out of frame can be glimpsed on the floor, wrapped in a black plastic garbage bag.

The figure goes off camera, returns and slaps a hunk of what looks like meat onto the black stone countertop. The chunk of flesh oozes, weeping an opaque fluid. The figure caresses the meat. The video fast-forwards as they place the hunk of meat on the cutting board and begin slicing off sections, more liquid sluicing out. When the playback speed returns to normal, the figure is placing the steaks in a Pyrex dish.

Next, they hold out sprigs of a dark green coloring to the camera. These go on the cutting board, still sticky with the excretions of the meat. The figure begins dicing them, taking time now to show the viewers how to grip the knife as high up the handle as they can, index finger pressing on the stem of the blade. They slice the sprigs, from right to left, then upwards. His arm is working like a piston, the blade whirring: an automatic guillotine.

He takes one steak and places it on the cutting board, rubbing the shredded herbs in, massaging both sides of the meat tenderly until it is stippled. The video speeds up again as this process is repeated for each of the cutlets. They are all placed back in the Pyrex.

The figure holds up a small burlap sack to the camera, tilting it to reveal a grimy gray spice. He grabs a handful and covers the meat with it, rubs it in, flips the meat and grabs more spice. Herbs and tombstone-gray mulch stick to the black gloves.

They hold up a transparent plastic bag filled with a beet-red marinade. The figure gives the sauce a close-up. It is chunky, almost gelatinous. A handwritten label stuck to the bag reads: LEAVE UNTIL CURDLED

The image cuts.

The camera is pointing downwards at a grill, outside at night, wood is burning bright beneath it. The flames and sparks rising with the smoke are the only light. The figure, their hood pulled up over their head, is scrubbing the grill with a half of something that looks like an onion, but it is hard to tell.

The steaks are thrown on, flipped quickly multiple times with a pair of tongs. The video speeds up again, the meat being tattooed with charry lines of ash. The fat and the sides are seared, the figure holding them directly over the flames one by one until they are all placed back in the dish.

The feed cuts again, momentarily.

It opens on a candlelit room. Cobblestone floor, puddles of wax, and wooden chairs. No table. The chairs arranged so that their backs are facing each other—the opposite of a support group—and greenish, tarnished dog bowls are positioned on the floor before each of the chairs. The camera pans down to gloved hands and a Pyrex dish. Tongs place a steak in each of the bowls, lingering— expectantly—on the close-up of each portion before it is deposited in the bowl.

The camera recedes showing the full scene: near empty room, chairs all facing away from each other, dog bowls filled with the carefully prepared meat.

An empty chair, untouched, slides slightly backwards.

Rare Caucus Steak with Exotic Herbs and Spices #initiation. 19 Views.

View comments

Bonitabambi_95: Men will literally fly to the Caucuses to grill meat rather than seek therapy. He's not bad with the knife tho, and his surface at least looks clean to start. Cant say the same for the ingredients. 3wks ago.

FridgeanWarlord: Dude has taken the 'Masculine urge to' meme to new heights. LOL. I wouldn't be cooking with that roadkill looking ass stuff. 3wks ago.

VinniePazStanJMT: Why the fucking algorithm thinks I need to see this? NGL steak looked good at the end. At the start not so much. 3wks ago.

LvCraft_CraftLvr: anyone else notice at 00:37 there is something moving in the sauce??? 3wks ago.

CaucusAesthetics: Want to say this is not food eating in Georgia. Come to Tbilisi to try real Georgian Khinkali! 3wks ago.

JOSmithsOnian: @ImissPenguinClub this is the one I was telling you about. Dude's making reels for Addams Family meals. 2wks ago.

> **ImissPenguinClub**: @JOSmithsOnian Food Network meets ARG. I'll wait for the Wendigoon explainer video. 2wks ago.

Dale Baran: I was struggling financially before I started trading with KreasCoin. The only crypto you can trust. Guaranteed to see return and growth. DM me for more details. #Crypto #KreasCoin. 2wks ago.

* * *

{*Profile Picture*}
Cooking_Alone@Night 2wks ago [Follow]
Auseil, France (Music: *Requiem for an Elder Oddity* by Erich Zann)

A fixed camera points down at a figure standing behind a kitchen island. The countertop is glistening black stone, there is a wooden cutting board and a large Damascus steel knife resting next to it; the overhead light plays on the stained striations of the blade.

The figure's face cannot be seen. The camera shows only their torso, clad in a plain black hoodie, sleeves rolled up to the elbows, exposing skinny arms. The figure is wearing black nitrile cooking gloves. An object just out of frame can be glimpsed on the floor, wrapped in a black plastic garbage bag. Torn sections of duct tape ribbon downwards, fluttering with a slight breeze.

The figure walks off camera, returning with a pallid, moist bundle, reminiscent perhaps of a cephalopod. Using the knife, looking unwashed, he bisects the creature, pushing the larger, fleshy section aside. He arranges the tumescent lengths on the cutting board and begins to chop them into rings. A caption pops up on screen in a black box with white text:

Not as fresh a catch as recommended but these are exceedingly rare. Was the Fishmonger who procured it for me. Not cheap. This recipe would not work with regular calamari.

The textbox disappears as the figure gathers the rubbery rings in both hands and places them in a glass bowl. He picks up one ring, inspects it. His hand goes upwards, disappearing from the camera's view. His hand comes back down. The ring is gone. The gloves are lathered in an oily substance; small, pale, fleshy pieces adhere to them. One of his hands reach offscreen, returning to view holding a glass jar. He holds it up to the camera, displaying a chartreuse-hued paste. Using his fingers, he scoops the paste out generously, plopping it into the bowl with the rings. Next, he mixes it all in the bowl by hand, tossing, twisting and squeezing. Kneading. Pressing. Kneading. Pressing. A pointed finger, dripping with the goo, goes up and off screen. When the hand lowers, that finger is clean, the light reflecting off the gloved finger, now wet with saliva.

The bowl, and the mixture it contains, is set aside. The figure pauses, seems to be looking behind them. The feed cuts for a fraction of a second. Continuing with the figure standing by the counter, the fleshy section of the cephalopod is now on the cutting board, resting atop yellowed wax paper. With a hammer he begins tenderizing the already flat meat. Turning it to pulp. Worms and wriggling parasites fly with each strike, others writhe and leak out from the fleshy head. The figure does nothing to clear them away. The textbox reappears: Don't consume these. Or do. Will not produce desired effects.

The figure has a burlap sack. They're holding it above the counter. They pour a dough-like substance onto the pummeled corpse of the creature. The concoction is kneaded and pressed by hand, then rolled with a conical stone that looks eerily similar to the stone of the countertop. The video speeds up as he rolls the stone, resuming regular playback when the figure holds up a wafer-thin sheet. He pulls a pasta press from off camera into view. It looks antiquated and rusted, but he cranks the lever with one hand as he feeds the sheet into the machine with the other. The textbox reappears: Has to be good and stringy.

The feed cuts and instantly continues over a pot of boiling water, the homemade spaghetti is thrown in. From this angle there is a better view of the thing wrapped in the plastic garbage bag. The textbox pops up: Don't stir. Do cover. Don't want anything getting out.

Next a pan is placed on an open flame next to the pot. The calamari-like rings, previously cut and left in the strange paste, are dropped onto the pan with a hissing noise.

The feed cuts again and opens up in shadows, only the light from the camera gives the viewers an idea of where the figure is now. The figure is now holding the camera, lowering it to a shallow hole dug on a sandy beach at night. The stone that had been used as a rolling pin stands at the center of the divot like an obelisk.

The camera is set down. The figure's bare feet can be seen walking past and then returning. They pour the water from the pot into the hole. He picks up the camera and shows himself tossing the pasta into the surf where ink-black waves are breaking. He returns to the hole and begins placing the calamari rings into the sand, pressing them into the sloping walls of the small excavation until they have lined the entire interior circumference.

The camera pans to the black nothingness, the expanse of night where dark waters and night sky are indistinguishable. The feed inexplicably stutters like an old VHS tape. The textbox reads: Bon Appetit.

Calamari á la Carcosa #initiation #visitation. 922 Views.

View comments

JamesMacAllister: First comment! Here I am with defrosted calamari, looking for a recipe video and my disappointment is immeasurable. WTF is this? 2wks ago.

ImissPenguinClub: @JOSmithsOnian new creepy ARG cooking channel just dropped. 2wks ago.

> **JOSmithsOnian**: @ImissPenguinClub what in the name of R'yleh is this man doing? Think Wendigoon or Nexpo have seen these yet? 2wks ago.

ImissPenguinClub:
@JOSmiths0nian probably.
They must be waiting for the
season or whatever this
dude's doing with this to
finish. Watched it a few
times now, so obv a Cthulu
thing, liked the first one
more TBH. Plus had to mute
the video cz of the music.
Was starting to feel
nauseous and not from the
guy's 'cooking'. 2wks ago.

LewisKim005500: *Posts the
Spongebob 'My Eyes' Gif* 2wks ago.

Sewer_Diverboy: @LewisKim005500
Post the Friends Gif with Phoebe
and Rachel screaming "My Eyes! My
eyes!" 2wks ago.

LvCraft_CraftLvr: Whatever is in the
trash bag definitely moves. Watch when
the Chef puts the 'pasta' to boil, you
can see it then. Also the duct tape was
clearly taken off and put back on from
the last video. 2wks ago.

Arkham&cheesesandwich:
@LvCraft_CraftLvr Saw it. WTF?
Also think this one is a bit try-
hard. Prev one was better.
Calamari a la Carcosa is a little
on the nose. Anyway saved the
video for when this inevitably
gets scrubbed. 2wks ago.

Bonitabambi_95: BEGGING people to
please clean their kitchen utensils
before cooking! Also mute the music
it's beyond trash. 2wks ago.

Alexia_Rafta_: It's like watching Trevor Henderson go on Master Chef. 2wks ago.

FridgeanWarlord: Anyone notice the location is different in both videos but the kitchen looks pretty much the same? Big Chad energy to not even clean the knife from last time. George Carlin would be proud LOL you got to exercise your immune system! 2wks ago.

MbappeistheGOAT: Comparing this to real French cuisine is like comparing Pessi's world cup career to Mbappe's. And yes, to the people saying mute the music, *c'est terrible.* 2wks ago.

VinniePazStanJMT: Man's tripping. Last video he at least made something that ain't look half-bad. This? Goofy shit. Soundtrack should go in that trash bag of his. Shit giving me a headache same as his food this time making me feel sick. 2wks ago.

Dat_MappausantGuy: This person makes his own squid spaghetti and then throws it into the sea? As if he's inviting someone or something from the depths. Not bad. Don't know what's up with this comment section, thought the music was beautiful. But can't find anything else by the artist? Anyone else have any luck? 2wks ago.

Rusty Coals: it's not really Calamari a la Carcosa unless it comes from the Calamari region of Carcosa. Otherwise it's just sparking squid feet. 2wks ago.

Rusty Coals: *Sparkling. Dammit. Ducking autocorrect. 2wks ago.

Jo3_B: Anyone notice the light in the sea right at the very end??? Trying to screenshot it but cant manage. Literally the last frame before it skips. 2wks ago.

Arkham&cheesesandwich: Back to say can't find Auseil on Google Maps. 1wk ago.

Dale Baran: I was struggling financially before I started trading Ambrosia. The only cryptic you can trust. Guaranteed to sea return and growth. DM me for more details. #Crypto #Ambrosia. 1wk ago.

VinniePazStanJMT: Get lost Dale, stupid bot MF. 1wk ago.

Alexia_Rafta_: LMAO. 1wk ago.

* * *

{Profile Picture}
Cooking_Alone@Night 5days ago [Following]
The Copper Still Taverna, Mitsero//Nychtapolis (Music: *Blackbird Crow* by Chambers of Catabasis)

A fixed camera points down at a figure standing behind a kitchen island. The countertop is glistening black stone, there is a wooden cutting board and a large Damascus steel knife resting next to it; the overhead light plays on the striations of the blade.

The figure's face cannot be seen. The camera showing only their torso – clad in a plain black hoodie, sleeves rolled up to the elbows, exposing skinny arms. The figure is wearing black nitrile cooking gloves. An object just out of frame can be glimpsed on the floor, wrapped in a black plastic garbage bag. Torn sections of duct tape ribbon downwards, fluttering with a slight breeze. The bag is clearly open, though what is within is out of view.

The countertop is filthy. Iridescent stains and watermarks have congealed upon the surface. The cutting board is warped, the wood looking soft and spongy; a few barnacles adhere to one corner. The Damascus blade refracts the light in ruddy hues, it looks sticky with a vermillion and ochre sheen.

The figure goes offscreen and returns with an aged copper bowl and sheets of phyllo pastry. He lines the interior of the bowl with the sheets, taking care to press them down against the copper surface, ensuring the pastry rises over the lip of the bowl. The textbox appears in the top right-hand corner, white text framed in black: A bag full of rye.

The figure bends down, out of shot, reappearing with a hemp bag. They go back under and come up with a pestle and mortar—both tarnished, green copper, inscribed with strange symbols.

He pours the grain from the bag into the mortar and begins crushing it. The video speeds up, showing him grinding the rye into a fine dust before adding more from the bag and repeating the process.

The video speeds up, faster, until it's a blur. The figure grinding and mashing the grain for an inordinately long time, pouring and pressing at an artificially dizzying pace.

When the video finally slows down, the figure pours the contents from the mortar into the copper bowl. He spins and rotates the bowl as if it were the dial of a safe he was manically trying to guess the combination to—clockwise by thirty degrees, counter clockwise by two-seventy, clockwise ninety, clockwise ninety, and then the video speeds up to a nauseating pace again, obscuring the figure's actions but again making it seem as if the process is going on for a far longer period of time than would be necessary or rational.

When the video resumes at a regular speed, the figure pushes the copper bowl off screen, then retrieves another old-looking inscribed copper pot. They place this on the countertop. The textbox reappears: Another type of rye. Compliments of The Still.

They begin pouring bottle after bottle of liquor into the cauldron. The feed is sped up again until the figure is done. Empty bottles litter the countertop. At regular viewing speed again, he pushes the cauldron aside, puts the cutting board in the center of the shot and goes off screen again. This time they return with a struggling black bird. The textbox tells viewers: Don't be alarmed. It's not a bird. Not really.

He uses the knife to saw off the wings. The not-really-a-bird battles in his grasp. Then he places the severed wings to the side and begins plucking the creature. The video cuts.

The figure is holding the camera directly over the first copper bowl. The featherless, wingless creatures are flapping nubs and stubs, trying to keep their beaks above the waterline of booze. The textbox says: the maid was in the garden/hanging out the clothes/when down came a little black bird/and pecked off her nose.

The figure reaches for the black garbage bag on the floor behind him, knife in hand. His back to the camera blots out whatever it is he is doing. Turning back around, he makes sure that the contents of the bag are not viewable to the camera. He places a clutched fist over the cauldron and drops something in. Then he places a lid over the mixture.

The screen fades to black. A text overlay says: wait. If you've followed the recipe correctly. You'll know how long.

A fixed camera points down at a figure standing behind a kitchen island. The figure takes the lid off the pot, begins placing the plucked and drowned birds into the other dish, until the pastry is brimming with them. The figure takes the pot and holds it up, tipping it to his unseen face, alcohol and blood run down his obscured chin and splatter his hoodie and the countertop.

Next he rolls a sheet of pastry over the pickled birds, sealing them in a pie. He uses his fingers to press down the crust, using the knife to make holes at the center. Holes that, from the birds-eye view he tilts the camera to, seem similar to the strange symbols on the copper kitchenware he has been using. He sets the camera to its original position and begins lining the edge of the pie's crust with the severed wings. The textbox materializes and reads: all that's left is to bake. Then serve. If you feel like you are being watched simply don't look back. Ignore. For now. Remember though we seek only to feed the Observationists this must be a dish fit for the Copper King.

The image cuts. The recording reopens but now the video quality is jarring, the picture grainy, flickering and distorted for the remainder of the playtime. The camera recording in night mode. The scene is still barely visible, almost all black. It shows the figure holding the pie, slowly approaching a plinth or altar. He places the pie in a depression set atop the plinth. Traces or outlines of other figures—far taller than the one who prepared the pie—flicker in and out of view, never moving.

He walks past the camera, out of view, then returns holding the garbage bag. He lays it before the plinth and begins to unwrap it.

A dainty dish to set before the Copper King #initiation #visitation #supplication. 100822 Views.

View comments

Alexia_Rafta_: what the actual EEEFFFF??!! Reported! 5days ago.

Jolande2000Steenhuisen: Disgusting!!! Those poor birds!! Why must people do things like this? I hope every person who sees this reports him! 5days ago.

StevefrmArlington: Honestly wtf is wrong with people? Sick sick! Tagging @PETA Also reported! 5days ago.

ImissPenguinClub: this guy's account about to go the way of Ghost Town Adventures. Speaking of, does anybody know how to get the metadata from the videos? If anyone does, better do it fast, looks like this vid is getting flagged and mass-reported. 5 days ago.

> **Arkham&cheesesandwich**: @ImissPenguinClub not saying I'm saving these but click here to anybody that wants to rewatch these after they inevitably get taken down. 5days ago.

Arkham&cheesesandwich: Anybody heard of the band this song is from? I don't like it, legit makes me feel dizzy (itchy?) but I can't stop rewatching just to listen to it. 5days ago.

JoziHustla: Straight up wildin! This some Zambian Meat Market ish. Haibo! 5days ago.

Landof_Milk&Hani: @JoziHustla str8 witchcraft shizz. Y u watching things like this? Worse mos, I like this song. Don't know why. 5days ago.

NAFO_Bogan_Boyo: Maybe nuclear winter isn't such a bad thing anymore #fella. 5days ago.

NfieldBrudda1046: Hold up let my mans cook. 5daysago.

LewisKim005500: Animal cruelty. Disgusting. Reported. 5days ago.

FridgeanWarlord: PETA virgins crying like they don't know where their soy-laden fast food burgers come from. This absolute BRO surpassed the Liver King and cooking on esoteric shaman levels. 4 days ago.

LvCraft_CraftLvr: My theory: Whatever is in the garbage bag is central to this. To what end I don't know—a vessel maybe? Or an entreaty to this Copper King? The first vid is the start of his journey, and leads him to the next and so on. Because at the end of each vid the Chef's presenting the food for someone/something else. So each "dinner guest" tells him what he needs to reach the next stage of the ritual…see more. 4days ago.

Arkham&cheesesandwich: @LvCraft_CraftLvr very interesting. To add to this, can't find this tagged location either or the band too, so did the Chef make or commission an original score for this vid and he's using a VPN or just making up the locations? 4days ago.

JOSmithsOnian: @LvCraft_CraftLvr That's a

pretty good theory, nicely done! This probably my new fav ARG, since Where is Gregory hasn't posted in forever, and Marble Hornets. I know the comment section is on fire right now, but it's obv staged…I mean it has to be, right? How else do those plague doctor guys (IDK) at the end keep flickering in and out? I kind of want it to be real. Does that make me a bad person? They're not really birds. 3days ago.

> **Bonitabambi_95**: @JOSmithsOnian No it doesn't make you a bad person if you want to watch someone mutilate LIVE BIRDS, not at all, cz afterall your horror feefies are all that matter. As long as you get your jollies. Fucking troglodyte. 3days ago.

Rusty Coals: Looking for tickets to this Paravani place in Georgia. It's a lake there. Found a connecting flight on an island nearby called Cyprus. Can't find the Tavern but this Mitsero has a lake too. Welp, guess where I'm going? Rocking soundtrack too, wish I could find more from these guys. 2days ago.

ImissPenguinClub: No search results for Nychtapolis but tickets booked for Georgia, flying out in a week. DM me anybody keen on joining or just meeting IRL. 2days ago.

LvCraft_CraftLvr: Nobody should try recreate this. 2days ago.

JOSmithsOnian: Can't wait for Wendigoon or Lazy Masquerade to make their own videos on this. I'll do it myself. Going to find this Tavern in Mitsero. Going on a little Eurotrip. 1day ago.

Dale Baran: Looking for cheap flights? I struggled to find affordable travel to the most exotic locations but with Omphalos you earn free points to make all travel easy and affordable! Omphalos the only crypt you can trust! #crypto #CheapFlights #Omphalos #Omphaloss #Omphalost 12hours ago.

* * *

{*Profile Picture*}
Cooking_Alone@Night

☹ This account no longer exists ☹ Click <u>here</u> to find out more about our <u>community guidelines</u>.

"DIGGING FOR THE DISAPPEARED"

Linda B. Adams

"There isn't any bus. This is bullshit."

I had to stop Ray from grabbing Tommy and punching him in the face. Or worse. Ray was the one who'd gotten us into this and Tommy always knew how to get under his skin. I wasn't sure if Tommy really did think it was bullshit or if he was just mad at Ray because we'd slogged through so much on our quest. We were dirty, tired, hungry, and dehydrated.

I pulled a strap hanging from Ray's backpack, causing him to nearly fall into me and crash us both into the muck we were wading through. But I saved him from getting at Tommy. Physically, anyway.

"You're a piece of shit, Tommy. The bus is real and if you didn't think so, you shouldn't have come."

"Like I had a choice," Tommy muttered.

He had a point. When Ray got something into his head, there wasn't much for getting it out. And because the three of us had been friends since grade school, when a bunch of older kids tied Ray to the merry-go-round and ran hard enough to spin it into little more than a metal, wood, and Ray-colored blur. Ray was the new kid, moved to Rutland Hollow from somewhere in Louisiana bayou country. This far into the wilds of New York, nearly within spitting distance of the Canadian border, folks didn't take well to unfamiliar accents and ways of being. That's the bad part of the Hollow. The good part, at least I like to think so, is the folks who'll look out for you once they decide you're worth looking out for. That was Tommy and me with Ray that day. We threw rocks at those older guys, hitting one square in the temple, causing him to fall and get tangled beneath his friends' feet. That forced the merry-go-round to a stop and one of the friends of the rock-to-the-temple kid said something about making Ray eat dirt for the trouble they'd found themselves in.

"Hadn't oughta," Tommy said. You gotta understand about Tommy. He's got an attitude, but he's also got steel in his spine that comes through in his voice. Those boys heard it and they took off running. Didn't matter that Tommy was nine. Didn't matter, either, that we didn't know Ray from Sunday. Tommy didn't stand for that sort of thing and that's why I stood with him. And Ray, too, from that day forward.

I tell you this so you'll understand why Tommy went along with Ray, and why I did, too. And so you'll understand why Ray sometimes had a glaring need to punch Tommy in a way that hurt. Tommy saved Ray that day on the playground, for sure, but he also tore a hole in Ray's pride that no amount of time could repair. Ray was caught in the spiderweb between gratefulness and resentment. It wasn't a good place to be, but I think it's why he dragged us into some less-than-sensible shit over the years. This search for the bus was just the latest incarnation.

Ray was into the high strange and he sought it out like a lighthouse that would save him from crashing on the rocks of himself. Tommy said Ray brought some darkness with him from the Bayou Country, but I told him that was some racist or elitist shit and I wasn't standing for either.

"I don't mean it that way, though. I just think some things get into your bones when you're from a place and it doesn't matter where you move to, your bones are the same." We'd sat at the base of a tree out in Mr. Rhinebeck's field, watching his cows graze and digging circles in the dirt for something to do.

"Like why we hang out in a cow pasture. That's a thing we do in the Hollow and maybe other places like it. But it ain't the same for kids coming up in other places. Like Boston. Or New York."

He had a point and I think it played a big part in why we went along with Ray on what he called the Bus Trip. Because wherever that bus was from, it wasn't from the Bayou Country, Rutland Hollow, or any place you can find on a map.

Ray first told us about it one day when we were hanging out at his house after school. It was early June and the endless ring of summer gathered around us, drawing us into the labyrinth of its promises. Our last year of high school waited at the end of it but we didn't want to think too much about what came after.

"You guys gotta see this," Ray said, firing up his laptop. "'Cause if this thing's real, it's, like, proof."

"Proof of what?" I asked.

"Proof that time and space are all fucked up."

"Back to the Future, y'all," Tommy said.

Ray entered his password without bothering to acknowledge what Tommy'd said, pulled up the *Banners of the Weird* website. Tommy didn't say anything, only rolled his eyes. I kept silent for reasons of my own.

BANNERS OF THE WEIRD

THE INTERNET'S FOREMOST FORUM FOR FORTEAN PHENOMENA

THE LOST BUS

Moderator8

Starting a thread here because I don't see anything else about it on Banners. Don't even see much about it anywhere on the internet, so checking with all you Bannerites out there to see what you've heard. Anything?

EsotericDeer

You mean the one that's supposed to be out somewhere in the wilds of NY?

SlappysTeeth

Totally craptastic, you guys. That bus is about as real as the tooth fairy. Cool story, but not factual. I think it started as a creepypasta

DreamsicleSun

I don't think so. I think it's legit. My uncle's got a friend who told him one of his friends found it. Somewhere way the hell upstate. Like far enough to make Syracuse seem downstate.

HomeworkEater9

Newbie here. What y'all talking about? What bus?

EsotericDeer

Hey, Homework. Welcome to the forum. There's supposed to be this bus way up near the Canadian border in NY that's from some school downstate. Which doesn't seem like much until you go a little deeper. Legend says there's a bus up that way that's over 400 miles away from its route in the middle of the woods with no sign of any passengers

HomeworkEater9
Like that Into the Wild bus? Up in Alaska?

DreamsicleSun
No. That one's got markings. And it's in a museum
somewhere now. They had to take it out of there 'cause
people were going to visit it and the rangers got sick of
having to rescue people. This bus is a school bus.
Supposed to be from Morgan Strait Consolidated School
District. Except if you look into it, there is no Morgan
Strait CSD in New York State. Or anywhere else

SlappysTeeth
Which is a pretty good clue that it's a bunch of shit. Why
would a bus from a school that doesn't exist be
somewhere in the woods hundreds of miles away from
where it didn't exist anyway? Seriously. WTF?

Moderator8
Hey, Dreamsicle, if one of your uncle's friends found it,
not sure he'd be able to talk about
it. If it's all true, anyway

DreamsicleSun
A friend of one of my uncle's friends

SlappysTeeth
Ah, the good old reliable FOAF. The ultimate red flag of
falsehood, staple of the urban legend

DreamsicleSun

Thing is, though, after my uncle's friend told him about it, he went with his friend to find it and my uncle never heard from either one of them again. My uncle and his buddy played poker every Friday with some other friends in my uncle's basement and they were working on an old Galaxie, trying to get it road-worthy. He wouldn't have skipped out on my uncle

HomeworkEater9

Maybe he owed money in the poker game

DreamsicleSun

Oh FFS, they played for pennies. Ain't nobody skipping town on account of that. What do you think this is, The Sopranos?

EsotericDeer

It's real. But it's not yellow like most school buses. It's the same blue as a robin's egg. And there's a key etched into the glass on the doors

Moderator8

How do you even know that, EsotericDeer?

EsotericDeer

Because I've seen it. And I never want to see it or be anywhere near it again. The fucking thing made my dreams all weird and gone to some hellscape. I'm not talking nightmares, I'm talking elsewheres. Like when I sleep I don't dream, I go to another place. Always the same place. And I don't want to be there.

I didn't even touch the bus. I swear. I'm sorry I ever went looking and I sure as hell wish I hadn't found it

SlappysTeeth
Oh, come on. You're saying it's real? You've seen it? Come fucking on

EsotericDeer
You don't have to believe me. Can't expect you to, since my phone crapped out on me when I tried to take pictures and I was stupid enough to go alone. That thing's so deep in no cell phone'll pick up a signal. Hell, I doubt even a personal locator beacon would work and they're supposed to work everywhere. The bus is real. Don't go. Don't look for it. I'm telling you. I wish like hell I hadn't

HomeworkEater9
What's the deal with it? If it's just a bus in the middle of nowhere, what's the big deal?

EsotericDeer
If you touch it, you aren't staying here. Not in this world. Or this dimension. Or whatever. I wasn't stupid enough to touch it, but I was stupid enough to look for it. I'm saying stay away. No, I'm begging you to stay away. I'm fucked up for life just from being near it. Just don't

SlappysTeeth
Whatever. Don't know why you're stirring shit up over something that's at best an urban legend and at worst a pile of steaming disinformation. It's just an internet story. God, y'all. Seriously. Chill the fuck out

EsotericDeer

Believe or not. But don't go. Don't look. Just forget it. Moderator8, burn this forum to the ground. Error404 it. Don't go digging for the disappeared

DreamsicleSun

My uncle misses his friend. Put up a FB page looking for information. About him missing

EsotericDeer

He's not coming back

#

So that's why we're slogging through the back country, looking for a bus that may or may not exist. Tommy thinks it's shit, Ray believes it like a religion, and I'm in the middle, stuck between my friends, agreeing with Tommy, but keeping my mouth shut.

"The black flies are thick as peanut butter out here," Tommy said, thrashing his arms around.

"I'm surprised they'd go anywhere near a sour ass like you," Ray said.

"I'm sweet as they come. But I'm about to go. As in back. I can't stand this heat, these bugs, and my balls feel like meatballs in molding broth. I love you like a brother, Ray, but your damn quest is gonna kill me." He stopped and turned around. "And for what?

Seriously? A fucking bus?" He slapped at a black fly on his face and turned around, huffing away from us.

"Go on back, then. We'll find the bus and tell you what you missed. And you'll be sorrier than a twelve-year-old without an iPhone."

"Fuck you and the fucking bus you rode in on," Tommy said, but he kept walking.

"What if it is real?" I asked, not knowing I was going to say anything until I did.

"Of course it's real."

"You owe me some serious shit for sloggin' through the bog, bro," Tommy said.

The woods were thickening, the brackish water beneath us drying up. We'd left the swamp about a half an hour ago, our clothes still wet from the waist down, duckweed clinging to our pants. My socks were wet through my boots and I could feel blisters forming on my heels. I was about to suggest we turn around, that Tommy was right, when I ran into Ray, who'd stopped as if he'd walked into a wall.

He pointed to something in the distance. "You guys see that?"

"Jesus," Tommy said. "What's there to see besides trees, trees, and more fucking trees?"

"Open your eyes, doofus. That's a lot of blue. Look." He thrust his finger toward something in the distance and took a step forward.

"There's nothing—" I started to say, but then saw the distinct turquoise of a robin's egg, large in the distance, like unexpected sky crouching in the trees. I suddenly felt like prey. I held out my phone and hit record, even as I remembered what someone had said about phones not working. Habits are creatures we feed.

"Holy shit," Tommy whispered, his voice laced with awe.

Ray took another step forward and we followed. He broke into what passed for a run between the trees, sending branches snapping and whipping at us. He let out a whoop that scared crows from the trees, which had gone the grayish-white of dead bark around the bus.

"Hold up," I said, not liking anything I was seeing. Not the bus, not the departing crows, not the skeletal trees.

Ray stopped and turned to look at me. "Seriously? We come all this way, trudge through some bad shit, get eaten by bugs and scraped by branches and you want to stop? Why the fuck'd you even come, then?"

I couldn't say it was because I didn't want to feel left out, that I'd sided with Tommy in thinking the whole thing was a lark, that it would just be another adventure we'd laugh about later, giving Ray a hard time for pushing us into it. I couldn't say any of that, even though it was true. I couldn't say it because I didn't like the look in Ray's eyes, like he wasn't my friend, but an imitation. It was then that I understood that Ray would've gone even if we hadn't, that the bus was his obsession, and I wondered how well I knew my friend, how well I'd ever known him. I shrugged, opting for silence, and Ray turned back to the bus and walked to it the way my mother had walked to the front of the church to receive communion every Sunday.

Tommy opened his mouth to say something and I shook my head. Whatever either one of us might have said at that moment would've been empty words falling against Ray's need to get to that bus.

We could still make out the words Morgan Strait Consolidated School District, but they had faded to a gray against the blue and before long they'd be lost to the sun's fading and be readable only if you knew that's what the letters were supposed to form. The blue, however, hadn't faded at all. We stood next to it, prisoners of our own thoughts, the only sound the faint wind in the leaves that had gathered on the ground, forming a bed for the bus. But none of the leaves touched the tires and none of the dead trees touched the bus. That it had been here for some time was obvious, which made it impossible for it not to be partially swallowed up by the forest's growth. Nature takes over everything.

Ray started toward it, his hand out.

"Don't touch it," I whispered.

Ray laughed and touched his tented fingers to the blue metal. I watched as they disappeared. Ray's mouth opened like a baby bird's waiting to receive its mother's offering, his silence tearing a hole where his scream should have been. I filled it for him, the raw pain of it ripping my throat raw. Tommy grabbed him and pulled, the momentum sending Ray falling on Tommy as the two of them crashed into the dead leaves, the sound like the breaking of tiny bones. I screamed again—or maybe I never stopped—as I watched the blood drip from Ray's hand as he looked at it, his mouth still wide and silent.

I watched as a key appeared on the bus's door then split in half as the doors opened. Ray winked out as if he'd never been there, leaving Tommy grasping for our friend who was no longer there. As the doors closed I finally heard Ray's scream and thought of that day on the playground as if our friendship had formed some mad circle that had meant to close in on itself all along.

Tommy ran for the bus's doors and before I could pull him away he pressed his fingers into the seal between them, trying to pull them open. I heard a wrenching sound as his arms were pulled from their sockets, the bus pulling them in through the small gap he'd made. Then he was gone, disappeared like Ray into whatever that bus really was, wherever it came from. His wire frame glasses thudded against the ground and I held in the crazy laughter that bubbled up into my throat.

I ran until I couldn't see the bus anymore. Until I could almost think I'd dreamed the whole thing except for the fact that my friends were gone. I thought of Tommy's glasses glinting in the sunlight by the bus either as a warning or a beacon, a dim part of me telling me I should go back for them and shoving the thought into the darkness of myself like a candle that had burned through its wax.

I trudged back through brackish water and forest, holding out my phone until I could get a signal.

#

BANNERS OF THE WEIRD
THE INTERNET'S FOREMOST FORUM FOR FORTEAN PHENOMENA

THE LOST BUS

SlappysTeeth
I'm sorry I didn't believe. Don't touch it. Don't go near it. Don't look for it. Forgive me. I'm going back for my friends. I gotta go back. Tommy can't see without his glasses

EsotericDeer
Hey, SlappysTeeth, don't do it. Please

SlappysTeeth
Tommy, Ray, and Alex. No better friends. Remember us

DreamsicleSun

Are you for real? You found it?

SlappysTeeth

...

BANNERS OF THE WEIRD
THE INTERNET'S FOREMOST FORUM FOR FORTEAN PHENOMENA

THE LOST BUS

Moderator8

I guess by now everyone's seen the video. Anyone think it's legit?

EsotericDeer

I think so

DreamsicleSun

I want to think so. I mean, if it's true it helps explain why my uncle's friend disappeared

Funland49

I think it's bullshit. It's just the sky through some trees and some doofus yelling and a bunch of crows cawing and flapping their wings. I could've videoed that at my buddy's hunting camp

Moderator8

I don't know. I don't know what to think

EsotericDeer
No sky is that color. Look back at the thread. SlappysTeeth said some pretty serious shit and changed his tune from punk to classical. He hasn't posted anything here in weeks

Funland49
Course not. He dropped that video like it was a mic. He shows up on the forum and bam! Story blows up like a headline on this place. Probably change his handle and be back on, if he hasn't already. Besides, we don't even see the bus. Why? Because you can't video what doesn't exist

EsotericDeer
The bus is real, y'all. So's the video. SlappysTeeth isn't changing his handle cause he's gone

DreamsicleSun
I showed my uncle the video and he wants to find the bus so he can find his friend

Funland49
Maybe Jimmy Hoffa's in the bus LOL

EsotericDeer
<file upload>
Look. I zoomed in and even though it's very pixelated, you can see the faded letters: MORG between the branches. That's not sky. That's a one-way ticket to elsewhere. Shut this forum down, Moderator8

BANNERS OF THE WEIRD
THE INTERNET'S FOREMOST FORUM FOR FORTEAN PHENOMENA

<search> blue bus Error404 the lost bus
Error404
Morgan Strait Consolidated School District
Error404

"TRANSCRIPTS OF SANDWICH REVIEWS POSTED BY DOMINIC STACHOWSKI BEFORE THE MURDERS"

Steve Loiaconi

Welcome to the Stacked Feed.

See, it's a little play on words, because I'm Stack and I'm gonna be feeding myself some things. This is where you'll get unbiased, unvarnished video reviews of sandwiches and burgers from all across the greater Ypsilanti region, without fear or favor. I'm talking delis, pizzerias, the little local joints, the big-ass chains—hell, any upscale fine dining establishments that maybe have a banger of a French dip on the menu, whatever. If it's between bread, we're gonna give it a shot.

So let's get down to it. Today, we're at Pop's Pizza on Main. I ordered up the chicken parm hoagie. Here it is, fresh out the kitchen. Look at that, globs of cheese sticking to the foil, steam rising up. Big old stack of napkins waiting for you in the bag, like a promise.

Now, here is my philosophy on the chicken parm: the cutlet needs to be crispy on the outside, not too thick, not too thin. You want a good amount of sauce, but not so much that it makes the bread all soggy and everything falls apart in your hands before you finish it. I'm looking for a decent cheese pull, but again, the chicken must be the star of the show.

Pop's, you players got some game. This is what I'm talking about right here. It could use maybe a bit more seasoning, a scooch less sauce. I prefer mozz over provolone myself, but to each his own. We're going to have to refine our rating system as we go, but I'm gonna say, off the bat, we're looking at eight stacks out of ten. Peace and hair grease, everybody.

***

Again, yo, I'm Stack — Dominic Stachowski — and it's time to get our feed on.

Note to self: this joint needs a legit theme song.

In the meanwhile, I got a real positive response to my last video. Some nice messages, a dollop of vitriol. One outright nutbar who thinks you should make parm with grilled chicken. Go back to Russia, DogLover88. A few questions that I just want to address at the outset here. I am not a content creator by trade. I'm not an influencer or a dudefluencer, whatever that is. I'm just a guy with a phone who likes sandwiches.

Until recently, I worked a real job, on the assembly line, eight hours a day, at the factory across town. Then the good people at General Motors decided my services were no longer required, to put it more politely than they did. I've been looking for work elsewise, but it turns out my skills aren't exactly marketable if you're not looking to build a mid-size SUV.

My wife Maggie, God bless her, but she got real tired of my unemployed ass hanging around our one-bedroom apartment all day. Hey, no offense taken. I smell pretty ripe some mornings. But you know this economy. Everybody can get a job except the people who need a job. Don't believe any of this four percent unemployment hoo-hah. It is hard out here for a pimp.

So after a couple months of getting jerked around by HR biz-natches with nothing to show for it, I said, hey, let's do a little experiment. I'm going to try to monetize what I really love to do: eating meat on bread. And lo and behold, I got me a shit-ton of views, started pulling in that sweet, sweet ad revenue, and baby, we're doing the happy dance.

Anyway, you're not here to listen to me narrate my bibliography. You're here for a review of the Burger King Angry Whopper. Straight up, I took two bites of this abomination, and let me tell you, if anyone should be angry, it's me, not the damn Whopper. Is this supposed to be spicy? And what's the deal with this cold, limp slice of cheese?

Now, I want to caveat this, I am not out to besmirch the humble minimum wage workers at the Ypsilanti Burger King. Peeps like them are the backbone of this country. This was a recipe handed down from some corporate hedgehogs, everything probably showed up in their kitchen frozen and ready to heat up and slop onto a bun. Disappointing. Two stacks.

***

It's the Stacked Feed. Feeding the Stack.

Yeah, no, that ain't it. We'll keep workshopping the song.

Hey, there's the factory where I used to work. Everybody give them a big two-gun middle finger salute. Automation and efficiency can choke on my ball-sweat. What about the dignity of an honest day's work, huh? Is that not worth something anymore in this country?

First off, I want to make one thing one-hundred percent Cristal clear: it's pronounced "ip-suh-lan-tee." I grew up here. I don't need some yo-yo in Albuquerque telling me the right way to say it. Yeah, BreakingBad69, I'm talking to you.

Also, SexySanchez1181, to answer your excellent question: tacos no, burritos yes.

To the rest of you who've been asking—deadbeat, loser, hobo, how are you affording all this food when you've got no job? Fair enough. I'll let you in on a secret. People like to say there's no such thing as a free lunch. I say there is, if you're willing to eat it on camera. You walk into Joey's Deli, tell Joey a couple hundred thousand people are going to watch you eat an Italian sub right outside, Joey will hook you up.

The old lady's been telling me I'm wasting time and money with this enterprise. I'm like, bitch, this is saving us money because I eat free every goddamn afternoon.

Speaking of which, Joey's Italian sub. You got your meats, your cheese—and here, I say, absolutely provolone it–tomatoes, shredduce, some seasoning, a dab of oil and vin. This might be controversial, but I do enjoy a little slather of mayo to balance it out.

Actually, excuse me. Correction. This is—get out of town—they put arugula on here instead of the old school shredded iceberg. I am deeply offended right now. I don't even know what to—it's fine. We're going to power through and judge the rest of the sandwich objectively.

Nope, nope. Can't do it. Three out of ten. We're done here.

***

Welcome back to the Stack.

Since I got laid off—which is to say, fired—I've been driving a lot. Just around town, up and down the strip, out into the hinterlands. Maggie, I say this with love, but she and I don't do well confined in a small space together for extended periods of time. So, you know, it eats up fuel, but keeping myself occupied is worth a few bucks a gallon for both of our sanity.

As I drive around and around, passing the time, I've been listening to some podcasts. You know, citizen journalists and former reality TV stars rocking the mics in their basements. I used to think they were all full of shit, but you close your eyes—and I'm not suggesting you literally do that while driving, mind you—it's almost like having a very chatty, somewhat paranoid friend riding shotgun. They might be scared the g-men are watching them through their toaster, but what they're not afraid of is asking hard questions with uncomfortable answers. I swear, a few hours can change your whole latitude.

Enough of that. It's chow time. This here is what's known as a Chicago dog. Mustard, relish, onions, tomatoes, a whole freaking pickle spear, and these things here are called sport peppers. Look here, I want to address the pink elephant in the room. Some people might say a hotdog is not a sandwich. Whatever. I say those people are broken in the soul. But see, the Chicago dog, it's kind of like deep dish, you get out of Chicago and nobody can do it right.

I don't know what's in the water down in the Windy City, but Marty's over in the Eastern Michigan U. food court, they can't bring that magic. Four stacks.

***

Stack here, and I don't even know where to begin today. The old mind-motor's been revving 24/7. The more I hear, the more I really pay attention, the more I find myself asking: what evidence is there that we're living in the real world? Like, is it a wild coincidence that stuff that happened on "The Simpsons" twenty years ago keeps happening today, or is some overmind plucking a smidgen of this and a soupcon of that from the ether of the collective unconscious and transmogrifying it? If every single one of us is trapped inside a carefully constructed dream realm, how would we know?

Apologies, folks, I haven't slept in a tic, my throat is desert-dry all the time, and I could not tell you with confidence when I last bathed. I'm sure Maggie thinks I'm losing it. It's in her eyes, these sinkholes of pity and doubt. She'd never admit it, but she lost all her respect for me a ways back. Now she keeps asking me what I'm listening to, what I'm thinking. She already knows the answer, but she wants to make me say it.

Why, yes, I am questioning the very fabric of our existence. Now please let me enjoy my Diet Squirt in peace, girl.

But see, another thing that's been needling into my brain, maybe I never got fired. Maybe I never worked at that factory at all. Maybe I'm a banker or a violinist on the outside. Maybe Diet Squirt isn't even a thing. The memories are so vivid, though. Technicolor, 4K HD. The smell of sweat and steel on the factory floor, the heat of the jig welders, the weight of the work gloves on your fingers. That feeling of satisfaction in your gut when a finished car rolls off the assembly line and you know your hands helped build it.

That has to be real, right?

No, Gr00tGr00t7, I'm not going to jump off a goddamn bridge to wake myself up and I'll tell you why. If you die in a dream, you die in real life. That's just science. It's like how two Ron Silvers can't occupy the same space at the same time.

So we do what we do. Carry on like the wayward sons we are. I've got a cheeseburger here from Bucky's Big Burgers, a double with cheese, bacon, onions, sauteed mushrooms, and their secret sauce. Everyone east of the Mississippi knows, the sauce is Dijon mustard mixed with Duke's mayo and sweet relish, but I won't begrudge them their air of mystery. What I do begrudge them is, this burger is a logistical fustercluck. You can't eat it. I take a bite at this end, half the toppings inside shot-put out the other end into my lap. It's too bad because the individual components are quite good.

Crispy bacon, smoked cheddar, no complaints about the mushrooms or onions. You just need a trough and a shovel to eat the damn thing, and that's disqualifying for a sandwich program. No rating.

***

I don't want to get sidetracked, but a bunch of you were asking about Ron Silver. Sit down and watch "Timecop." It'll all make sense.

Another question I keep getting—yo, Dom, if this is a dream, whose dream is it? Well, I'll tell you. This kid across the street here, this is Sammy Abromowicz, ten years old, lives in Ann Arbor. We're all inside his head. Looking at him, I don't even know if he knows it. There he goes, stepping off the school bus, running to his mother's arms, not a care in the world.

I've been following him for the last couple of days, charting his movements on this map, staying just out of sight. You wouldn't suspect a damn thing if you didn't know what to look for, but he has a unique aura, a sort of gravitational pull. See how the compass app on my phone goes haywire around him? Don't worry, I am on this kid like white on rice.

No, CashCookieXX, that is not racist. It is a factual statement. Rice is white. Unless it's brown, I guess. But "like brown on rice," that seems more problematic somehow.

Real quick, today's sando, it's a Balboa from the Ypsilanti Tavern. Rare roast beef and S   wiss on garlic bread. I used to love these growing up, or the me in here remembers that he did. The trick is, the meat has to be so rare it's practically bleeding. If it's overcooked, the sandwich is too dry. This one, I ate most of it on the drive over here, but I can assure you, they hit the sweet spot. I'm gonna say nine out of ten stacks, with a little extra credit for nostalgia.

Anyway, smash the like button, click the new donation link, buy me a cup of coffee. You wouldn't think one would need money or caffeine inside a dream, but here we are.

***

Something's not right. I keep seeing shadows. My internet connection's cutting in and out. The temperature in the air is shifting. The ley lines are all out of whack. My hair is growing faster than usual, but my fingernails are growing slower. Today, I tried on every single shirt in my closet, and six of them are suddenly too small.

Alright, Dom, Dom, Dom. Breathe. Don't bug out again.

Truth be told, yo, I don't have much of an appetite today. But I'm logging on anyway because I was studying up last night after Maggie conked out watching her *Sex and the City* reruns and I had a bit of a revelation. Now, I want to be sure we're all on the same page: you're not crazy. You saw that movie where Sinbad played a rapping genie, the one we can all remember the poster for in our heads clear as day but nobody can find a copy of it anywhere. Here's why: it came out in the real world 25 years ago and freaking 10-year-old Sammy in Ann Arbor doesn't know about it because he's got no goddamn culture.

The good news is, more and more people are seeing through the veil because of piles of incontrovertible evidence like I got in this folder right here.

Look, up in the sky. That airplane there, it hasn't moved in five minutes. Those trees across the road, that forest, you zoom in the shot like this, you can see the leaves are painted onto the landscape, impressionistic-style. Now, close your eyes and open them real fast, do it a few times in a row. Like, blink, blink, blink. What do you see? Did you see the face spliced between the frames of reality? It looks like Brad Pitt, doesn't it?

The cracks are getting bigger.

***

Apologies for the darkness, folks. I had to vary up my schedule because Sammy's minders are on to me. His little dream Gestapo in the Ypsilanti PD costumes don't quit. So today's review is going to be more of a midnight snack situation. We're at the Taco Bell off I-94, which thankfully is open late.

Here's what I've been trying to explain to Maggie about the dream hypothesis: it's fundamentally unprovable, right? The dream is fluid. The dream can adjust to explain away anything you or I might find suspicious, and we don't know any other reality to compare it to. Oh, fish can talk now? Sure, don't you remember it's always been like that? The only way to prove it is if we all wake up, and at that point, it's kind of moot.

Trust me on this. I'm no scientist, but I've heard knowledgeable dudes who have spoken to scientists lay it out many times.

Those flashing lights on the highway are too close for comfort, so let's cut to the chase: the Taco Bell grilled cheese burrito. I think they just took a regular burrito and melted some cheese on top, but it's not bad for what it is. The fiesta strips give it a nice crunch. You really can't tell that they used reduced-fat sour cream. You can add guac if you're looking to splurge.

I'm going to be generous here and say six stacks. Let's skedaddle.

***

Okay, check this: either the length of my nose keeps shifting by micrometers, or someone is messing with my ruler—and I think we all know who that would be. That's right. I see what's happening, Sammy. You're not fooling me. Not fooling anyone anymore.

Hold up, hold up. I guess he is fooling some of y'all. I'm seeing some real skeptical comments in the chat, and don't get me started on Maggie yapping at me back home. I've laid out the proof for you, pointed you to authoritative sources. I don't know what else you want. I mean, if this isn't a dream, how do you explain the giant fricking spiders?

Speaking of which, if you're still here for the sandwich reviews, I want to apologize. We've gotten waylaid from our primary objective here. I've got a lot going on. I'm prepping my go-bag, loading up the back of the CR-V with supplies. And hey, another thing, why aren't I driving an American-made car? I don't remember buying this foreign piece of crap. And this yellow, it's like I'm Colonel Mustard driving around town with a bloody candlestick and Mr. Boddy's corpse in the trunk. This is not a car the real Stack would have voluntarily procured.

Are you tripping, CosmoNut911? What do you mean, what spiders? They're all over Paris. I've seen the videos. Eight-legged freaks climbing the Eiffel Tower, laying eggs on the Louvre, spinning webs across the Champs-Élysées. Look it up. Go on. Remove whatever manufacturer-installed sensitivity filters are on your browser, go to one of the real search engines–none of that sanitized Google or Yahoo corporate crap. Type it in, "giant spiders France," and take a gander. Abre los ojos, por favor.

***

They killed her. They killed her.

Shit. Is this her blood? My blood?

One thing at a time, Dom. What I remember is, we had a big fight. She screamed at me, I said some things I wish I could take back, everything escalated and escalated, and then she told me we were for-real done. I thought maybe she meant it this time, but it doesn't matter. The sun came up this morning, I woke up on the couch holding this paring knife, and she was lying on the bathroom floor with her goddamn throat slit.

When did we get a paring knife?

Oh, what do you think I did, MonCapitanOblivious? I ran like a bat outta Compton. I heard the sirens getting louder and louder and I got the hell out of there.

I don't think I'm going to be able to pick up a sandwich today, fellas. It's not that I'm not hungry, but the true grit of it is the Five-O is looking for me all over town. If you sent me a donation in the last three, four days, I will refund you when I get a chance. You're not getting what you paid for and I don't need that hanging over me while I deal with this nonsense.

But I'll tell you what: when we get out of this hellscape, I'm going to set up my shingle and get back to it, hardcore. We're going to head up to Detroit. We'll travel the whole state. If there is a sandwich worth scarfing, it shall be scarfed. Assuming I live in Michigan in the IRL, of course.

Let's make a commitment right now, wherever we are when we all wake up, I am going to get my hands on a six-foot sub, half Italian, half American, and I am going to sit down and eat that mofo, live on camera. As long as it takes, and you're welcome to join me.

For now, though, this might be TTFN. Like a bee in a daiquiri, I got too close to the truth and I am drowning in the rum.

You might be next. They know you've been watching. Head on a swivel, yo.

****

I'm coming for you, Sammy. You hear me? Nowhere is safe. As my sainted grandmother would say, it is go time, shitbird.

Even if I wake up, she's going to be gone, right? Dead in here, dead out there. Everything is coming apart at the seams like a Chipotle burrito after a few bites. I can feel it, the dread in the pit of my balls. I haven't slept in two days. I haven't eaten, haven't showered.

I still have blood on my hands.

My cousin hooked me up with this Glock. I've been doing some target practice, shooting up cars in the old factory parking lot. I'm ready to take this fight to the source. Are you even ten years old, you little prick? Or are you like 75 and dreaming you're back in—hell, what year is it really?

Think about this, guys, we could be in the past or the future. We could all be living in another century on another goddamn planet.

I regret to say we're going to have to shelve the six-footer, but here's what I can promise: I will hunt you to the very ends of this Earth, Sammy, to where the ocean drops off into the eternal abyss of the abstract mind. I will find you, and I will place this gun against your head, and you will wake up or I will blow your little dreamy brains out your astral ear canal.

So let's go, Sammy. You and me. Mano a mano.

Maybe we both die. Maybe nobody wakes up ever again. I don't care anymore.

Game on, punk. Game on.

"A PLACE WHERE THE SUN HAS NEVER SHONE"

C.J. Dotson

"Daniel, come out right this instant!"

"Danny! Please! Please, Danny!"

"What the hell, Jacob, are you filming right now? Christ, put your phone down."

"No, you don't understand." Jacob's voice is rough, almost wild. "We need to have a record of what the fuck is going on here, we need to—"

His wife Rachel thrusts an arm out at him, jabbing her finger more than pointing. "Jacob Graham, I told you to put that fucking phone down now!"

Jacob lowers his phone, the dim twilight view of the Bluebird Lake Campground hiking trail swinging into a blur before settling shakily on a rocky dirt path and two pairs of muddy, well-worn hiking boots. The view doesn't go dark because he doesn't pocket the phone, doesn't turn it off.

Rachel doesn't lower her voice. "You're such an asshole," she says, and it's not like every other time she's said it, not like in all the videos when she's startled but laughing and playfully batting at him. She's practically snarling. "We talked about this! I thought you understood!"

"Baby, please." There's a desperation in his voice, and half the livestreaming (and, later, the recorded replay) commenters will say it's clear that this is the voice of Jacob Graham himself, unaffected and real and not the voice of JakeyJokes, while the other half will respond that this is just JakeyJokes leveling up his prank game for Halloween and pulling one over on his fans too, and this will not be the most replayed part of the video but it will be the point where most commenters agree that the changes in the forest have started.

It begins with the quality of light. Still dim and cool but less the blue of dusk, more purple. A bruise-purple, they'll argue, not a sunset-purple. There are striations in the dirt of the path, too, shallow and sinuous grooves that were not there earlier in the video. And when one of the Graham kids mutters a barely-audible "gross," people who have watched the footage in its entirety will look back to this and wonder what might be changing that doesn't come through in video or audio. The smell, maybe, or the temperature.

"This was your last chance, do you know that?"

"You're wasting time!"

The phone swings up again, the hiking boots and the reddening rocks leave the frame and the trees come back into view and they don't have as many leaves as they did a moment ago but on the first viewing most people will miss that because the phone is shaking in JakeyJokes' hand and his voice is shaking even harder as he repeats himself, louder, harsher.

"You're wasting time!" The view shifts as Jacob turns and then the movement comes to an abrupt stop and he says, "Let go of me. *Danny!*"

"*I'm* wasting time? No. You've ruined our Halloween campout with this bullshit." Rachel's voice is hard and uncompromising and run through with something between fury and sorrow. "You need to get this through your head: the videos are done. The channel is done. I'm not out here because you got me, I'm out here to find Daniel and ground him for going along with this after we talked about planning this shit instead of springing it on me."

The longtime fans (mostly teenagers) and the first-time viewers (many and varied after replays of the livestream go viral) will argue about these words with vitriol all out of proportion to the subject. Had JakeyJokes always been faking his pranks—was this an attempt to cover it up? Maybe he was going to start faking his pranks. Perhaps he only told his wife he would so she wouldn't suspect the next practical joke (and a sub-thread of commenters will argue with particular viciousness over whether or not this is abusive).

In the background the rustle of the wind is dying off and a teenage girl's voice mutters, exasperated and almost inaudible, "About time. His channel sucks anyway."

The view on the screen leaps away from the trees, flashing past Rachel, to settle on JakeyJokes' two younger kids. Adison is the mutterer, barely into her teens and dressed up in a standard Halloween-store witch costume rather than one of her many oversized hoodies. She's the target of as many of her dad's pranks as her mother has been, and she stands with her arms crossed and one eyebrow raised. As soon as the camera settles on her she rolls her eyes. Behind her, her younger brother Peter, dressed as a pirate complete with a smudged, painted-on five o'clock shadow that resembles dirt more than stubble, grins at JakeyJokes and gives him a thumbs up. Behind the both of them another flurry of leaves fall away without making any noise at all.

"Stay close to me," Jacob Graham says. His daughter rolls her eyes again and sighs loudly, and his son gives an exaggerated wink, and the trees pale so very slightly, and Jacob says, "I'm not kidding this time, drop the attitude and stay close."

Between the softening susurrus of the leaves and the fading calls of birds and bugs and Adison's explosive, "Ugh, *fine*," a sound builds. Viewers will be unable to agree on when it began or what direction it comes from or what could cause it—some animal, some audio artifact of wind and the way Jacob holds his phone, some speakers hidden in the woods by JakeyJokes—but they'll all agree that the low, long, somehow meaty sound is hateful.

The kids draw nearer and JakeyJokes' free hand comes into view, pulling his daughter's shoulder and then grabbing his son's cheap pirate vest, herding them closer still. He grips Adison's trailing, spiderweb-patterned sleeve and says, "Hold your brother's hand."

There's a confusion of voices for a moment. In the same breath, Jacob says "Don't step off the path" as Adison says "Wherever Danny's hiding he's got Rocky, so what if we just whistle and yell *treat?*" and Peter says "Where's Mom?" and the low, hateful noise rises for one second so that in the video everyone gasps and in their homes the viewers yelp or jerk in their seats or congratulate themselves on not getting jump-scared.

The camera pans up and down the path and Rachel is gone.

The leaves are gone, the bracken and grass withering. The trees are whiter still. Deepening redness seeps almost imperceptibly into the stones and the dirt.

"Rachel! Rachel!" Jacob shouts. The camera lurches forward as he stumbles down the path. "Rachel!" He's screaming now, and there's a rustle of fallen leaves, scuffing of shoes on dirt, breaking of twigs as his kids follow behind him. Their voices come through in bursts of intelligibility, bickering but not yet frightened.

"What is that smell?" Peter says, gagging.

"Oh, god."

The motion stops. The noises all die. The light is less purple and more red now, and the dirt and the stones are not just red but a black-red and the earth gleams. The trees have no leaves and no color, bone-white but not sun-bleached. This is a place where the sun has never shone.

The stillness and silence stretch on just long enough that some viewers will wonder if something has gone wrong with the livestream, if there's a problem with their app or with the video itself, and this will be the second-most paused point in the video.

Adison breaks the quiet.

"Jesus, Dad, drop it!" she shouts, coming into view as she stomps around the path to face her father. "We're not stupid, okay? There's no such thing as monsters. I figured you out! Stop acting like you're tricking anybody! You left Rocky tied up somewhere on his leash and made up that story, Danny was in on it, he pretended to go find Rocky — he knew exactly where to go, and now they're both hiding." She turns away from her father, toward the death-white trees and the bloodshot sky. She storms down the path, the ground slicker now and ropey, the gleaming black-red of it giving beneath her feet.

"Adison!" Jacob gasps. The camera jumps forward. He hurries to catch up to his daughter. "I said stay close!"

"Mom!" Adison shouts into the bone forest, her voice high but thick. Betrayed. "I can't believe you're going along with this! Just come *out* now, you guys! I don't wanna miss the lodge's costume party!" She pauses on the path, her head turning slowly back and forth, as if the thought of Bluebird Lake Lodge, glamorous under any circumstances and currently decked out like a gothic haunted mansion, has by contrast alone finally caused her to realize how different the woods have become.

"Dad?" Her voice wobbles. "How are you doing this?"

"I'm not doing anything, Adison!" The viewers who have never had children will think that JakeyJokes' shout in this moment is too much, too angry, bordering on violent. Most viewers who are parents will understand the frustration in his voice, even some of those who pretend not to. And they'll all hear his quaver of terror.

Great acting, they'll say.

Something terrible is happening, something real, they'll say.

"For real, how are you doing this?"

"Adison, think!" Jacob grabs his daughter's arm, tries to turn her to face him, but she yanks herself out of his grip. "Think!" he repeats. "How could I do all this? Look at the trees, look at the ground. Look at the sky, Adison, how could I do this? The hiking trail goes somewhere it shouldn't—somewhere wrong—and the thing in this forest—" he chokes off, then draws a shuddering, gasping breath. His voice softer and broken, at once heavy with grief and sharp with self-hatred, he says, "Fuck,

I should've gone to find Danny alone—but your mother would've worried… Your mother, oh god…"

Adison whirls on her father, the dawning fear in her eyes highlighting her fury rather than diminishing it. The fans and one-time watchers all agree that she looks like she's starting to get scared, looks like she's holding her anger like a shield against being afraid. They can't agree on the nuance—is she afraid because she's realizing it's real? Or is she afraid because JakeyJokes stuck to the bit and finally got her with his prank after all? Is that awesome, is it hashtag-parenting-goals, or is it child abuse?

She draws a breath as if to yell at her father again but instead she looks past him. The ground is made of guts now, the trees of bone, and veins pulse through the sky.

"Where's Peter?" she says, her voice much softer than it had been, the shrill harshness gone.

The camera blurs as Jacob spins and no one viewing will be able to pinpoint when the forest of bone and gore grew so dense. No amount of watching or rewatching will lead to any clarity.

Peter is gone.

"Daddy?"

Adison whispers the word in the single instant before the sound screams through speakers on phones and TVs and laptops.

The fleshy, hateful noise no longer permeates the background, but roars.

It drowns out everything else in the video. Drowns out any answer Jacob makes as he turns again.

The view trembles and stutters, blurs and refocuses. Between flashes of black, images resolve themselves in fleeting, racing-heartbeat instants:

Adison's face, mouth stretched in a scream no one will hear over the roar, eyes open wider than human eyes should bulge—

A pulse throbbing through the arterial sky—

The bone trees closing in—

The fleshy, intestinal earth rushing up to meet the fallen phone JakeyJokes records all his pranks on—

This will be both the most replayed and the most paused moment in the video.

As the phone falls spinning through the air, it catches the barest glimpse of something tall, something at once sharp and pulsating—all hunger without teeth or maw, all hatred without eyes or thought.

Adison stands halfway inside it, her back and her legs sinking out of sight, her head tilting further and further back. She reaches out, hands grasping, desperate. The substance of the creature crawls over her neck, her cheek. Fills her screaming mouth. But her eyes still stare.

A half-second later the phone lands face down, and the next five hours of the livestream show nothing but blackness.

There are links to articles about a family disappearing on Halloween night. The names match, the pictures match. Faked articles? Photoshop? Fake links? Bluebird Lake Campground and Lodge denies any hikers reported missing on their premises. The police organize no search, but internet sleuths and cryptozoology enthusiasts show up in droves for the rest of that autumn, with a brief resurgence in the spring, and they link to their blog and vlog posts about it in the comments.

Some fans living in the vicinity of Bluebird Lake, mostly teenagers and many of them hoping to pull some killer pranks of their own, begin planning weekend trips or asking their parents for visits to the campground. They will all go out on the hiking trail, following JakeyJokes, reveling in the idea of being in on his most famous prank ever.

Most of them will come home.

"BORROWED TIME"

Jason Fischer

Awakened from a fitful sleep in the hospital's private waiting room, John's eyes welled with tears when he saw the video. On an old-fashioned television, his girlfriend, wearing a terrified expression, paced in a very dark room, calling his name.

At first, he thought someone had brought a video monitor into the waiting room. That was until he realized Kim didn't look mangled or have tubes in her mouth as she did now. She was as pretty as he remembered her before the accident. The cobwebs of sleep made it hard to understand what was happening.

"What's this?"

A hooded man standing next to the square TV on a wheeled cart was silent. Squinting across the dark room, John saw a mirror image of the room where the man's face belonged. It was like he was wearing a foggy glass as a mask. Panic spread, layering John in sweat.

"Kim, what's going on? Can you hear me?" He knew it wasn't possible. The TV was hooked to an old VCR, but he asked anyway.

Kim's image grew sharper on the fuzzy screen. "John, where are you?" Her hand slowly crept forward and then halted, like a mime's, when it drew near the square television screen. "I can hear you, but where are you? What's going on?"

Her gaze fell on his, bringing a bright smile. "There you are. Of course, I can hear you. Why wouldn't I be able to?"

Because you have a tube down your throat in the other room. "Honey, how do you feel?"

The smile disappeared. "Empty."

The hooded man finally stirred, pressing pause. Kim's image twitched as the squiggly lines of the glass screen encapsulated it.

John jumped up, getting a head rush from lack of sleep and nutrition. The last twenty-four hours had left little time for either. Since he had received the call that Kim was injured, John had sat there, uselessly watching the hospital staff prod and poke the person he cared about more than life. Only the insistence of the nurses that he leave while they ran tests had forced him out of the ICU.

As John took a step forward, hoping he could stay upright, Kewell, the night nurse, entered the room. Her scrubs were a wrinkled collage of kittens. "John, you need to come with me."

She had been with Kim the whole time. Even after working a double shift, her face remained warm and bright, echoing her positivity. Being continually this close to death somehow didn't seem to penetrate those who worked there. They all went about their duties like factory workers, moving from one task to the next, oblivious to the seriousness of their actions.

"Why?" In the corner of John's eye, the shadow man was rolling the TV cart out the service door at the back of the waiting room. Still not fully awake, he fought to shake the fogginess from his mind. The urge to go after the shadow man made his legs twitch. Kewell's sharp voice sobered him.

"John, please listen!" Tracing his gaze, she glanced toward the closing door. It made her face bunch up as she stared curiously at him. "John, you haven't much time. She's awake."

"What? The doctor said that wasn't a possibility."

She held up both hands in a halting gesture. "Don't get your hopes up. It isn't like that. This is…it."

The tone of her voice confirmed his fears. A wave of nausea coursed through him, settling in his stomach, constricting muscles so tight they ached. "Oh, no." He took a step back as if he was trying to physically protect himself from her words. John's voice cracked as he said, "Please, no. I need more time."

"John, I'm sorry, but you don't have it. Let's go now. These lucid states generally don't last long."

It was as if a switch was flipped inside him. Cold crept over his skin, and everything began moving in slow motion as he followed the nurse, who had been so kind to him, into the death room.

An hour later, feeling everything and nothing, John returned to the waiting room, collapsing onto a fabric chair. Kim's sweet face as she closed her eyes for the last time hovered in his mind, bringing a heaviness that John had never before come close to experiencing. His fingers were trembling from the phantom memory of her flesh going cold as he held her. The reality he could not face set deep into his bones. Everything was now forever changed, and the one person who could help him cope with that was no longer there.

His nervous system was out of balance, sending equal waves of nausea and adrenaline through him. He knew he should begin making calls—their few friends had a right to know—but the thought of any movement brought exhaustion. Resting his chin on his chest, he could smell a trace of her strawberry shampoo on his t-shirt. He placed his hand on his chest, wishing he could hold on to that smell forever.

Not believing any of this could be real, he noticed a folded piece of paper sitting on top of his coat with the hospital's letterhead at the top. His first thought—that it was a bill from the doctors—made his face flush, and he wondered how they could be so callous. Swiping it up, he wished it was just a bill. On the note, in scribbled handwriting, it said:

If you want to see your girlfriend again, come to the sub-basement, Room Two.

Thinking of the man with the TV brought his eyes to the service door at the end of the rectangular room. His heart thudded quickly, paused, and then beat quickly again, as if to make up for lost time.

John clutched his chest, trying to retrieve his stolen breath. Each attempt was like sucking air through a narrow straw. Remembering Kim answering him when he spoke to the image on the TV, he stood. His heart pounded in his ears, causing a dull ringing. Something inside tried to stop him from walking to the door, trying to protect him from what had to be false hope, yet he went anyway.

Assuming it would be locked, he gripped the knob. When the door opened, relief ran through him. Tucking the paper into his pocket, he continued down a narrow hallway to a service elevator. The tight space reeked of cigarettes. Wondering who in their right mind would allow smoking inside a hospital, he clicked the down arrow.

Jumping when the service door sprung open, he expected the man to be there. But the dirty interior was empty. Stepping inside, he pressed the button below B, labeled SB. The doors, like massive jaws, swiftly shut before the elevator vibrated into its descent. He clung to a safety rail, trying to fight the disorientation.

The hardwood planks on the floor had dried stains littering the aging wood. Imagining bleeding humans on gurneys, he pressed himself against the walls. The vibration from the elevator's movement grew so strong his teeth were rattling until the compartment halted. There was no *ding*, only the creaking sound of gears grinding as the door slowly opened. The hallway before him was very dark. Reaching into his pocket for his phone so he could use the flashlight, he realized he had left it in the death room.

Sticking his head out of the elevator, he called out, "Hello?"

There was the echo of his voice and a dim humming noise in the distance. John took a small step out of the elevator, leaving one foot inside; the sense the elevator would leave if he took it out brought a chill. "Hello?"

Holding his breath to cancel all noise, in the darkness, he thought he heard static coming from the narrow hallway. "This's insane." He had glanced back at the elevator when he thought he heard her voice.

"John?"

His stomach dropped, and his back began to tingle. "Kim!"

"John!"

He took a step into the hallway, towards her voice, and the elevator door snapped shut. He screamed, "Honey!"

He took a breath and turned to walk into the darkness. Each short step activated something deep inside. John hugged himself and said, "Please, whoever's there, come out."

"John, it's so dark here."

Finding courage, he came to a corner. Peeking around, he saw two open doors. Light flickered through the one furthest from him. Taking calculated steps, he looked into the room closest to him. Inside was a waiting room with couches that were very low to the ground. He stepped inside and immediately began sweating. The room was several degrees warmer than the hallway. It stunk of tobacco and dust. Off in the corner, a woman with soulful eyes sat glaring at him. The fluorescent lights above flickered across her face.

Swallowing his fear, he asked, "What is this place?"

"The place where hope dies."

"What?" In the other room, he heard Kim call out again. His thoughts were moving too fast, making him dizzy. "Please, tell me where we are."

"Don't keep him waiting. It won't be good for her." She lowered her head, staring at the grimy floor.

He walked out and went into the next room. The walls were covered in rows and rows of VHS tapes in sleeves. On each bowed shelf, a piece of masking tape showed names printed in marker. In the center of the space was the flickering TV with Kim trapped inside. Her hands were pressed against the screen, the barrier keeping her inside the square. With darkness surrounding her, she looked like she was inside a house, staring out from a closed window.

"John!"

He froze, staring at the person he loved more than anything in the world.

"Honey, where are we? Why can't I get through?" She slapped at the screen.

The grief, mixed with panic, was making it hard to focus. Logic finally fought its way back. This had to be a hoax. "Kim, how many fingers am I holding up?" He made a peace sign with both hands.

"John, this is no time for playing, I'm really getting frightened. I can't get out of this…this space."

"How many fingers!"

Her eyes were wide ovals as she answered, "Four."

The little energy that was keeping him upright evaporated. Slumping forward, he walked to the screen. There had to be hidden cameras somewhere, and this woman only resembled his girlfriend. He didn't know how or why, but the thought would not allow excitement. Whatever hope he had left inside him tried to stop the next question: "Where did we meet?"

"John, why?"

"Please, it's important."

"You found my dog and answered my ad. We met at the coffee shop on Eighth Avenue, and then you took me out to dinner."

"What did you eat?"

"John, why?"

"Please, just answer!"

"Grilled cheese with fried pickles. Why are you asking this? John, what's going on?" Her nails scratched at the screen.

Knowing it was her, he took a swift step, placing his hand on the screen. Static from the glass tingled his fingertips. "Kimmy." His heart felt like it had turned to liquid and was dripping away.

She placed her hand against his, the cool glass preventing real contact. "What's happening?"

Inspecting the cart for a hidden camera, he nearly soiled himself when the hooded man stepped forward from the shadowy corner.

"Mr. Balsum. I would recommend you pause the tape." The voice was obstructed, sounding as if something was stuck inside the man's throat.

"Who are you? How're you doing this?"

"I promise to explain once you pause."

Kim screamed, "Who's there?" She leaned forward, looking for the voice. The glass distorted her face.

"When the tape runs out, she will be gone forever. Don't waste precious seconds. Hit pause *now.*"

Not knowing what to believe, John pressed the pause button. Kim froze with her mouth wide open. The image flickered, and it appeared like she was winking. His insides ached as if he had swallowed shattered glass. Gripping his midsection, he pleaded, "What's happening?" The man took a step back, moving deeper into the shadow.

"I took a video of Kim's essence just before she passed. Now she lives on inside the tape."

John looked over all the tapes covering the walls. Each label was a person's name. Images of hundreds of souls trapped inside the rectangular cases floated through his mind. "This can't be."

"Yet it is. I've given you what so many would love: borrowed time."

"How?"

"It's not for me to ask such things."

John peered, trying to make out the man in the shadow. "Who are you?"

"You may call me Mr. Iblis."

"Why do you do this?"

"I've answered enough questions!" His deep voice echoed in the darkness. "You must choose now."

"Choose what?"

"Play the tape until its end and spend another few hours with her before her soul leaves this plane. Otherwise, she will live on forever in the limbo of the tape."

"I don't know how you're doing this, but you're insane." He shook his head. "This is insane."

"Call it what you will; it doesn't change the result."

As unreal as it seemed, John knew what the man said was true. He asked, "Let's say somehow that what you are telling me is real. Why would I leave her trapped like that?"

"For many, it's better to know that their loved ones are not gone forever, especially considering you don't know where they are going." He turned, staring at the tapes and waving his hand at the shelves. "If you choose to leave her here, you may come back and play the video in increments. I must warn you, though, that there is no telling how long the tape will actually go, and once it runs out, she will be gone forever."

John stared at the strange man's hands. The fingers were of varying widths and lengths, none matching the opposite hand. His blood heated, rushing to his face. "This isn't fair. It's not for me to choose this!"

"Then press play and leave. When the tape ends, the eventual thing will happen."

"I…I…can't do this." He made tight fists, forcing his nails into his palms, hoping the pain would pull him from what he desperately hoped was a dream. Nothing changed. "Other people are in these tapes?" He pointed to the wall of shelves.

"Yes." Iblis stepped closer. His face was layered in VHS ribbon. The tape sculpted over his flesh. "You don't have to choose just now. I've plenty of space." He smiled a reflective smile, his tape tongue jutting from his lips.

"This's insane." John, no longer able to handle the growing fear, backed out of the room. Iblis lowered his hood. Seeing the reflective film covering his head made John's stomach churn.

When he passed the waiting area, the fragile woman was standing in the doorway, inches from him. "Are you done now?" Her eager eyes pleaded. "Is it my turn?"

He noticed two of her fingers were missing. The desperation in her eyes made him take a step back. "Why are you here?"

"Same as you." She rubbed the area where her flesh was gone. "To see my Stephen." Her eyes went to his hands. "Is this your first time?"

He nodded, trying to process everything.

"Don't worry. We all pay in our own way. It isn't as painful as you might think."

From the other room, there was the sound of static, followed by Iblis's booming voice. "Mrs. Novak, you may come in now."

She pushed past John and entered the room. There was a hitch in her step, making her movements stilted. John slowly turned, thinking of heading to the elevator and leaving this horrid place. Something compelled him to enter the waiting room. Exhausted, he sat on the aging couch. Next door, he heard a tape eject, then static. It was quickly replaced with the woman pleading, and then her shrill scream.

Knowing he couldn't leave, he hugged himself tightly, thinking of seeing Kim again and wondering what the price would be.

"DOPPELGÄNGER"

Kathy M. Bates

"Hey, wanna take a look?" the street vendor's mellow tone urged. "We got some new stuff in. Lots of specials. Real cheap."

I'd seen him before. Every few days, sellers lined West 3rd in an open flea-market fashion. Most tables were always there; others came and went as stock fluctuated. Mondays were the slowest but also the best time to get choice selections from whatever the vendor might have found over the weekend.

Tape Guy, as I came to know him, sold all sorts of things. I found his table by accident. It was off to the side, practically in the alley—part of the collective but not. I liked that he was different, not just with his location but his stuff. He boasted the most variety from estate sales, rummage sales, flea markets, and from the smell of some things, straight from the city dump. But if it was useful, in decent shape, and you were buying, Tape Guy was selling.

"Five," he shouted, hoping, I was sure, that his voice would reach past me and into the busy thoroughfare. "Five bucks for three tapes."

Like a boundary wall against the encroaching Beanie Babies, tower-stacked VHS tapes bordered half of one six-foot table, and more sat spine-up, lining the middle. Most were famous titles, with a few unmarked tapes sprinkled throughout for variety, especially in the center.

Who would buy a tape that had no identifying information?

And for the poorly labeled ones, who would buy someone else's random video recording? Anything—and I do mean anything—can be captured, hidden under plastic coatings, trapped on magnetic tape. The concept intrigued me.

Prisoners were left behind—on a VHS cassette, no less. Like most technology, analog tape cassettes had a lifespan, replaced by something newer and better, something more efficient to produce and distribute. Replaced and eventually dead. These abandoned artifacts fascinated me, especially those without discernible markings beyond the manufacturer's tag. Damaged stickers and haphazardly torn labels left the remains a complete mystery. It was a curiosity wonderland ready to be explored.

He was selling, and I was buying, the three-for-five special like a sugar-coated gateway drug. I remember the first tapes I bought: four labeled and two unlabeled. He even hooked me up with a player.

I knew I had one somewhere in the closet, in a box, behind a dozen other boxes that looked exactly the same. I took the bundle. It was practically a steal.

It took me a while to get around to watching them. Not sure why. Maybe it was a type of delayed gratification. I didn't know when I would be back downtown. What if I started watching them early, went back for more, and Tape Guy didn't show up with the goods? After a while, I couldn't hold back. Weekend or not, I started the show.

The first tape had a partially torn label, the only visible letters spelling the obvious.

T…V…SHOWS…

Reruns, or what would be reruns now.

The original owner, or at least the one who recorded them, had pressed the button at just the right time to catch the black screen seconds before the familiar title sequence played, a heartbeat's wavelength to prepare me for the performance as it was unveiled. Theme song, title—it was like I relived watching it for the first time.

'90's nostalgia at its finest.

The second cassette had no label at all, or if it had, age or rubbing alcohol removed all evidence of one's existence. The tape itself didn't look damaged. In fact, it was clean. Too clean. It could have been blank, for all I knew, until I popped it in the VCR and eagerly pressed *play*, ready for my next hit.

It was a school swim meet. I remembered those. A dad loved that kid enough to haul around an oversized camera bag with a clunky recorder and tape set inside. I can't even pretend to say mine would have done the same. Maybe that's the first thing that drew me in.

Everyone in the stands cheered, the camera holder and surrounding family the loudest voices by far, and not just because they were the ones closest to the mic. I bet people could hear those excited shouts for Matt a mile away, or at least from under the water's surface, where the boy glided mid-lap between the agitated waves.

He looked young—five, six, maybe? I pressed pause a few times and tried to focus on Matt's face when he stopped to smile awkwardly in response to the praise. He reminded me of one of my friends when I was that age.

"You can do it, Matt! Atta boy! Go for it, son!" All the love and pride and hope—family unity bleeding over mediocre basebands.

Beautiful memories, right? A family heirloom. Dad should have passed that tape on to Matt when he had a family of his own. Maybe sooner. They could relive family moments when would-be swim star Matt chased his Olympic gold dreams. Where was Dad now? Mom? How many brothers and sisters let Matt down by not sharing this nugget of youthful wonder?

I didn't know who to blame, but did it really matter now?

No. I was here for Matt.

It wasn't just one swim meet, either. One after another, Matt grew up before my eyes in back-to-back, ten-to-fifteen-minute bursts. The moments reminded me of my friend; even more, it was like seeing another version of myself. Maybe I was his age at the same time. If so, I might as well have been in the stands growing up alongside him. He grew faster, stronger, but most of all, happier, and so did I.

Matt's early years were innocent and shy. He rose high, fell hard, and swam back up again until they chanted his water swagger presence across the family and fan-filled stands again. You needed a bit of cockiness to survive, and he had it, fists balled, raised to the ceiling at the end of lane four, heat after glorious heat.

At the same time, failure did him a favor. He had a slump, somewhere around his pre-teen years, losing back-to-back. Dad still caught every second like it was the last drip of honey from the comb to sweeten the world.

How did something that precious end up in a pile of tapes sorted somewhere between a worn-out copy of *Risky Business* and Blockbuster's Special Edition *Dances with Wolves*? It scared me to think that Matt was abandoned. The ones that leave you behind are the real monsters.

My Matt views repeated so I could linger in the stands with our once-happy family, until I worried about the sturdiness of the tape strip.

The tapes weren't in the best shape to begin with, weather and time-worn to the point that black-and-white static lines interrupted a few of the intros, smooth, clear playback replaced by split-second shaky frames and sounds as the first thirty seconds of the show's time marker ticked by, and then a few more spotting the middle sessions. But I needed to see them. Situated in the stands, parked between Mom, Dad and siblings, I was part of the family—my friend Matt's family. What if there were more tapes with more families to welcome me with smiles and open arms? Others with moments to share, pulling me into a place of belonging?

What was I waiting for? I had more tapes. I started in on the labeled ones, discovering they were marked correctly—surprised that I found myself disappointed. I went back to Tape Guy for more, but that second time I studied his merchandise, choosing wisely.

The home-recorded tapes were where the rush hit hardest, labeled or not. But the others had the same chance to delight me. Without titles, even if they had video store stickers, I might get the genre, release date, or some tidbit to fuel my curiosity, like a retro version of a blind box. You know the style but not the exact one. Then people might buy more and more, hoping to collect all of them. Maybe what made them hand over their hard-earned money time and again had only part to do with collection completion.

What if it were more about exhilaration? Something known and not known mingling to produce tangible seconds of adrenaline. A real Schrödinger's cat moment—the worst-case scenario and the best scenario, what you wanted and didn't want all trapped inside a sealed, opaque container.

It had to be the rush or something like that to make the buyer not even bother to wait till getting home to find out which number the out-of-the-ten-possible they got—sitting in the car, cautiously opening the box not to cause any damage, taking out the prize, pressing fingers into divots, trying to solve the mystery. Then, dramatically ripping into the deluxe-grade silver foil wrapper inside between hungry teeth.

Win. Lose. Both. Heart racing to elation, depression, or an unsettling middle ground that left a taste in the mouth that screamed for one more bite.

Hungry, I lost count of how many times I shopped the tapes. Then they became part of my routine. Matt was my first friend like that, and I never wanted to forget my first.

#

"Matt," the barista shouted above the bustle of a packed coffee shop. I almost didn't hear them call out and might not have noticed if it weren't for the name I knew almost as much as my own. His name tickled the edges of my interest even over the people-cram around me.

A busy lobby wasn't unusual for this time of day, the 8.30 a.m. rush before city professionals strolled into their 9-to-5s. I didn't speak to anyone, not even the clerk, as I pointed to the 20 oz coffee special on the small chalkboard in front of the register, paid, and moved to the waiting zone. I kept to myself, and they to theirs.

"Matt! Tall white chocolate, extra shot, no foam, no whip."

I couldn't help but scan the crowd, hoping their Matt was my Matt. How many years had it been since the last recorded swim meet? How old was my best friend now? Mid-to-late twenties? This guy fit that bill. Especially since his clothes were Gap-ad-sharp enough to shave some years off—not all of Matt's swim meets had a time and date stamp. But I remember one of them showed 1996; he could have been in his early teens. Swim Matt was Caucasian, clean-cut prep-style, with dirty blond hair in messy, heaped curls before they were tucked into the swim cap. This guy fit that bill, too.

His eyes could have been any color: the VHS images weren't that sharp, and none of them ever got that close. But I imagined they were blue, maybe as deep azure as the pool water he loved so much.

Instead, the way to tell—the smile. Swim Matt had the biggest smile, a supernova that exploded through the natatorium, one recording after another. Then, after a while, I saw myself in the stands, absorbing the energy, wave upon glorious wave.

We were family, he and I.

He must have heard his name and walked toward the call. I waited for the smile. He picked up his beverage and nodded across the counter curtly. I still waited. He grabbed an extra napkin from a nearby condiment station, all while I waited. Patiently at first, then not so. Where was it? His face was flat, lacking expression, as imageless as the blank parts of the videotapes mixed into the copied ones.

Maybe something was wrong.

Frustrated, I followed him out of the store and down the block like a mad scientist searching for an escaped lab experiment, fascinated that it might be him and curious about where he'd been all these years. Eventually, he disappeared around a corner, lost to me.

I returned to the coffee shop regularly, sometimes seeing him, other times not. I watched his movements, and more questions arose with almost each encounter. Where was his family? How did the VHS tape with their beloved son end up in the hands of a stranger?

But then again, I wasn't a stranger. Not anymore.

If Dad, Mom, Sisters and Brothers weren't there for Matt, I was. If this was how they were going to be, I didn't need their help to be Matt's newest cheering section, his biggest fan, even if I was the last one left.

But something seemed off. Reunited with Matt, even from a distance, he'd changed. I watched my favorite meets before going to the coffee shop. Maybe I searched for clues, needing to find differences from then to now. Even the smallest one could be the breakthrough. But the thing I was most concerned about—today, Matt didn't smile. I watched and waited for weeks, and the smile I wanted to connect with so fiercely stayed hidden. Maybe it was there just under the surface, but sadly, not even a hint of one ever came through.

From the tape to now, I found a few variances. Age: I couldn't help with that one. Family: finding them at this point might be trickier than working with what I had at the moment.

But there was one main, glaring difference. I couldn't believe I hadn't recognized it from the very beginning—the water! I saw Matt on the street, in the coffee shop, and even trailed him to various nearby locales, but we never made it far enough to a public pool. Matt was never around the water. Was that why he couldn't smile anymore? Did he miss swimming and being around water so much that it affected him emotionally?

I could work with that. If anybody could help, it was me, Matt's best friend and most loyal fan. That's what family is for.

I had to do something. I kept an eye on him for a few more weeks while I hatched a plan to bring the smile back to Matt's face.

Lesson learned: Archimedes, with his fulcrum and lever, was far more optimistic than me. But I made it happen.

Another lesson learned: chloroform can be purchased, but practical use is all jacked up. The movies have it all wrong. It takes at least five minutes. Five long, torturously hard minutes. But again, I made it happen.

Matt was lying parallel to the pool's edge when he woke up. I picked a gym with an indoor pool that hardly anybody used during the day, no night classes, and no cameras. Safety and security must have been the first budget cut, upkeep on door locks included. At night, not even the cleaning staff stuck around for long. It was tricky getting in, but worth it.

Matt looked at me and blinked, eyes glazed. I put a comforting hand on his shoulder. I'd already untied him. All he had to do now was allow his mind to return to the last moments of pure happiness, return to better days, surrounded by friends and family, and most of all, the water that connected us all. Waking up took longer than I expected, but he came around.

Groggily, he shook his head toward the water and grunted a few times. I patted his arm. Smiling, I followed his eyes to the water, then waited for those baby blues to meet mine again. As soon as they did, I knew the time had come. I stretched my lips across my teeth enough to mimic a smile we might have exchanged at the closure of the best swim meet of our lives.

His eyes widened, and I nudged him until his body met the water.

He sunk into the pool, continuing to wake up. Limbs stretching, he continued to look at me. The smile was coming. I'd set his comeback up for success. The pool was just like one from his early days. All it lacked were the cheering stands to one side. I should have spent more time looking, but at least the water was clean and clear. Whatever the location lacked, I would make up to Matt, like a one-person pep squad leading him back to his best life.

His body made ripples in the water, but no waves.

This was it!

My Matt, the one I'd missed so much, the one from the tapes, was only seconds away. I imagined being closer and putting myself beside him as the water gently enveloped us in familiarity. I relished the thought that he'd returned to his beloved home after a long parting—two separated halves becoming whole again.

This was it. This was our moment.

A rush of—something— Comfort? Gratitude? I couldn't put my finger on the sensation as I waited, this time sure to be favored with Matt's whole-hearted smile of thankfulness. I was the one to reunite him with his one true happiness. That should mean everything!

Then, a rush of something more. Fear? Adrenaline? Matt hadn't changed his facial expression in the slightest, not since the last hair on his head dipped below the surface. As he sank, the water was still clear enough to maintain mutual eye contact.

Something wasn't right.

The Matt I knew was an excellent swimmer. If anyone would fall to the bottom and rise again, it was Matt. In fact, he might even propel up, victory-balled fist with all the water swagger months ago I'd only dreamt of seeing up close and personal. Matt never failed me. Not then, and not now. I had to believe that.

Others might drown. Others might give up. Survivalists understand times like Matt's journey to the bottom. The questions your mind ventures to ask—fight or flight. The emotional push and pull on your psyche. The soul is willing, but the body is weak. From childhood, Matt was of like mind in both.

Instead of drowning, instead of letting the panic and terror overtake you, all you have to do is wait. Take a deep breath, stay still, and hold it; wait for your body to sink, wait for your feet to touch the bottom, and then make a decisive leap. Push up toward the surface and survive the terror-rush imprisonment back to freedom. If you're going to drown, it's better to fight, better to leap.

All Matt needed to do was push off from the bottom.

"Push," I shouted. "You can do it, Matt."

He stared at me, eyes wide, unblinking, from eight feet below. No fight, no panic, the only thing down there, and the only thing between us—emptiness.

"What the hell is wrong with you? I did all this for you. Now fight through like I know you can," I screamed downward, hoping it would penetrate the water. I remembered one of the fans once said something similar. They cheered for the swimmers to overcome the struggle and come out on top. Fans, friends, family, and the crush of the rally pulled them together like a string tied together at the ends.

But he didn't push. Strangely, he wasn't struggling that much either. Worst of all, no smile. Not a single tooth. Matt never smiled, even surrounded by the water I thought he'd loved so much. Not once. His struggle under the water was gentle, like he had given up before the fight even began. This was not my Matt. This was someone else's Matt. An imposter meant to mislead me.

My Matt was still out there somewhere.

My Matt still needed to be saved.

"A KING IS NOTHING WITHOUT HIS QUEEN"

Angela Sylvaine

@KING95
June 2nd at 10:31 a.m.

Hey

June 3rd at 4:03 p.m.

Hey pretty lady

June 5th at 11:07 a.m.

Hey beautiful you know you can do better than him right? You need someone who treats you like a queen

June 6th at 8:54 p.m.

He wanted you to wear that didn't he? Red is a whore color and you have more class than that

@1MOLLYMAE
June 7th at 7:06 a.m.

What the fuck dude?!? I don't know you! Leave me alone!

June 7th at 7:08 a.m.

How did you know I was wearing red?

June 7th at 8:15 a.m.

Seriously how?? Answer me!!

@KING95
June 8th at 9:01 a.m.

Thought you wanted me to leave you alone

June 8th at 9:05 a.m.

Don't worry I'll never leave. It's not right the way he talks to you

June 12th at 11:17 a.m.

That white dress was for me wasn't it? It's perfect just how a woman should dress

@1MOLLYMAE
June 12th at 12:08 p.m.

Where are you?? Are you watching me??

@KING95
June 12th at 2:54 p.m.

Always, my love, always

@1MOLLYMAE
June 12th at 2:57 p.m.

Please just leave me alone

@KING95
June 12th at 3:01 p.m.

And abandon you? Never

@1MOLLYMAE
June 13th at 6:02 a.m.

Tell me your name. Your real name! I know it's not King

June 13th at 6:04 a.m

It's not fair that you get to see me and I don't get to see you!!

June 13th at 6:10 a.m.

What do you look like? Send me your picture

@KING95
June 14th at 1:02 a.m.

You have seen me

June 14th at 1:14 a.m.

You see me every day

@1MOLLYMAE
June 14th at 5:45 a.m.

Where?? Who are you?? Tell me!!!

@KING95
June 14th at 5:52 a.m.

Don't worry, it won't be long now

@KING95
June 17th at 9:23 a.m.

HOW DARE YOU BLOCK ME
YOU UNGRATEFUL BITCH!!!

June 17th at 9:32 a.m.

How did it feel to have that officer laugh at your report? A restraining order? For what? For saying you're beautiful?

June 17th at 9:52 a.m.

I know it was him that made you do that.
Pretty boy motherfucker

June 17th at 9:57 a.m.

Don't worry. I forgive you

@1MOLLYMAE
June 17th at 10:01 a.m.

How are you even doing this??!

June 17th at 10:07 a.m.

How did you know about the cop?!? I was alone when I called them!!!

@KING95
June 17th at 10:12 a.m.

You're never alone. I'm ALWAYS here for you

June 18th at 8:32 a.m.

Hey beautiful

June 20th at 9:08 p.m.

It's good he's gone. Don't be sad. You're prettier when you smile

June 20th at 9:14 p.m.

With him gone we can finally be together

@1MOLLYMAE

June 20th at 9:23 p.m.

What did you do to him???

June 20th at 9:25 p.m.

If you hurt him I will kill you. Where is he??

@KING95
June 20th at 9:29 p.m.

You're just upset. I didn't hurt anyone

@1MOLLYMAE
June 20th at 9:31 p.m.

He's missing I know you did something

June 20th at 9:32 p.m.

Please just tell me where he is!!!

June 20th at 9:34 p.m.

I know you fucking did
something to him you sick fuck!!

@KING95
June 20th at 9:36 p.m.

Stop saying that! I didn't do anything!

@1MOLLYMAE
June 23rd at 5:18 p.m.

I know who you are now

June 23rd at 5:21 p.m.

You thought I didn't see, but I caught you looking at me in the elevator doors and saw that dumb fucking crown tattoo on your arm KENNETH

June 23rd at 5:23 p.m.

And I'm not going to let you get away with this

June 23rd at 6:03 p.m.

Did you hear me call the cops this time you stalker asshole?!?

@KING95
June 23rd at 6:05 p.m.

I DIDN'T DO ANYTHING!!!

June 23rd at 6:07 p.m.

Leave me alone!!!

June 23rd at 6:08 p.m.

I don't know what happened to him

June 23rd at 6:09 p.m.

Please answer me!!! Help me I need you

June 23rd at 6:10 p.m.

Please. Answer me

June 23rd at 6:11 p.m.

I'll leave you alone, okay? I will.

@user3796213569
June 28th at 8:17 a.m.

Hey

@KING95
June 28th at 8:21 a.m.

Who is this?

@user3796213569
June 28th at 8:22 a.m.

Thanks

June 28th at 8:23 a.m.

You were right. I could do better

....

THE DENVER POST
Man Arrested in Connection with Cherry Creek Murder

The man accused of killing a 31-year-old investment banker pleaded not guilty to murder charges in Denver Superior Court following his arrest early Wednesday. Authorities found the victim, who'd been stabbed seventeen times, in a Cherry Creek dumpster.

Police identified the suspect as 29-year-old Kenneth Aaron Ward, who had been previously reported for stalking the victim's girlfriend. The alleged murder weapon was found in Ward's vehicle.

In a statement made through his attorney, Ward proclaimed his innocence and insisted he was framed for the murder. During this Thursday's arraignment, he was ordered jailed without bail pending an upcoming court appearance.

"MOTHER OF BLOOD"

E.S. Huberty

"Do you remember the game *Mother of Blood*?"

Jay knows the question comes out of nowhere, but as soon as his sister walked into their apartment, he couldn't hold himself back. His sister Cyprus blinks at him for a second.

"Well, hello to you, too," she says, kicking off her shoes. "My day was fine."

Jay shakes his head a little, trying to shuffle his chaotic thoughts back into place. "Right, sorry." He nods toward the card table where they eat most of their meals. "I got dinner. Chinese."

He waits for Cy to get settled, practically vibrating with impatience. Once she's at the table and chewing peanut sauce noodles, he asks the question again.

She squints one eye, her fork hovering over the white takeout box. "Maybe?"

"It's like *Zork*," Jay continues, dabbing orange sauce off his chin with a coarse paper napkin. "You remember *Zork*?"

Cy rolls her eyes. "Yes, Jay, I remember *Zork*."

Jay knows it was a dumb question. Any gamer worth their salt knows that game. While it's completely text-based, his mind still conjures a picture of the iconic white house with the front door boarded up. Using nothing but a keyboard, his imagination, and a guide, he'd spent hours exploring the ruins of an underground kingdom collecting treasure and solving puzzles. Landing on the right turn of phrase was like casting a magic spell.

"Okay, okay." Jay mimics his sister's eye roll. "My bad. Anyway, *Mother of Blood* came out in 1980, but it totally flopped. Like no one played it. My friend Adam had a copy, though."

"Wait..." Cy spears a head of broccoli. "Oh my god, I think I do remember! You were kind of obsessed with it, weren't you?"

Jay grins. "Mom hated it. She said it was too scary for kids."

"I can't imagine why, it sounds so cute! What's it even about?"

Jay sets his fork down next to his plate of chicken and spreads his hands dramatically. "You're looking for your sister in the woods, but then you stumble upon this abandoned cabin. As soon as you get inside, the door locks and you're trapped. To get through each room, you have to solve puzzles. As you explore, you pick up clues about this lady whose kids got killed." Jay scratches his head. "It starts out awesome, but the ending…it's like famously bad. After you solve like three room's worth of puzzles, the front door opens and all you can do is leave. That's it. You never find out what happened to your sister or what's up with the lady and her kids."

Cy scrunches her nose. "Well, that's not cool at all."

Jay nods in agreement. "The creators tried to justify it with some shit about the chaos of grief and the mystery of life, but that just pissed people off more."

"And you liked this game?"

Jay's grin widens. "I remember staying up really late at Adam's house trying literally everything to get a better ending. I was sure we were all missing something big and the developers would, like, give out a prize if someone figured it out."

"But no one did."

"Nope. And then, because the game was such a dud, the developers ended up shutting down completely. *Mother of Bood* never got remastered or remade, so it's been nearly impossible to find a copy you can still play 15 years later. It's like it just vanished." Jay runs a hand through his tangled curls. "But I've been searching forever, and it turns out I'm not the only one who spent hours looking for an alternative ending."

Cy smirks. "You weren't the only dork, you mean?"

"Oh, you're one to talk, lady," Jay exclaims. "How many hours have you spent just *listening* to video games?"

Cy straightens in her metal folding chair. "I want to be a voice actor, Jay. I'm honing my craft."

"Right, right. Anyway, I found this forum where a guy claims he figured out which puzzle triggers the other ending. He wrote down the commands, but since it's practically impossible to find a playable copy, no one's checked if he's telling the truth." Jay tents his fingers. "Until now."

***

The bulky monitor squats goblin-like on the desk, a snake's nest of cables and adapters coiling in and out like life support. When he hooked everything up, Jay half-expected it to start smoking right then and there. He strokes the top. "She's not a looker, but she's got *Mother of Blood* on the hard drive. Please don't ask how much it cost."

Cy takes a step back toward Jay's unmade bed. "Should I ask about the viruses it's probably sending to every piece of technology in the building?"

"You know that's not how that works." Jay pulls up one of the cushy computer chairs and pats the back. "Come on, you gotta be curious, right? Will you play with me?"

Jay's heart races as he waits for his sister's reply. Finally, she sighs. "Okay, but if this thing catches me on fire, you owe me a new outfit." She slaps her thigh. "These are Guess jeans."

Jay pats the chair again and grins. "Deal."

***

```
You are standing in a big, empty field.
The safety of home lies behind you. In
front of you waits the thick darkness
of the forest. You hear the cries of
crows. The forest is dangerous. No one
goes into the forest.

> go back home
Your sister went into the forest. No
one else is brave enough to look.
You're the only one who can save her.

> go into the forest
You enter the forest. The air is cold
and sweet with the smell of decay.
Thirty years ago, a woman disappeared
in the forest. Her children had been
sleeping in the field when a plow cut
off their heads. When the woman heard
what had happened, she murdered the
plowman and carried her children's
severed heads into the forest. Do you
hear the crows?

> listen to crows
The crows sound like children
screaming.
```

```
> keep exploring forest
The forest looks just as it appears in
your dreams. Fog wraps around the tall,
old oaks and cloaks the ground.
Branches hide the sun, turning the
forest dark as night. In your dreams,
there's always a cabin.

> look for cabin
You see the cabin. It sits in a
clearing near a tree stump. There's an
axe in the stump.

< take axe
The axe handle breaks off. You are
defenseless in the forest.

< walk toward the cabin
The cabin windows are black with grime,
blocking the view inside. In your
dreams, the door is always unlocked.

< open cabin door
The door opens.
```

***

"Hey, I gotta pee," Cyprus says suddenly, pushing her chair back.

Jay stretches his arms above his head and winces. He's been so focused on tracking down this game, he hasn't slept much, and when he does, it's usually on the lumpy couch in the living room. His neck is paying for it. "Okay, I'll wait for you."

"No, no, you keep going," Cy says. "I'll just be a sec."

She disappears into the dark hallway. Outside, an ambulance paints the window red for a second. Its wail reminds Jay of a giant bird. He considers waiting for Cy anyway, but when she takes longer than two minutes, he turns back to the computer.

***

```
<enter cabin
You step into the cabin. The
floorboards are uneven and soft with
mold. A large picture in a gold frame
hangs on the hallway wall.

<look at picture
It's a grainy black-and-white picture
of the cabin. A woman is standing in
the doorway holding an axe, her long
hair hanging like strings of seaweed on
either side of her face. In the
background, two small figures look out
the cabin window. Their faces have been
smudged out.
```

***

"Hey, Cy? Hurry up! Things are about to get good!" Jay calls. He pushes his computer chair from the desk and peers into the hallway. The only light is the sliver beneath the bathroom door. "You're not scared, are you?"

"Ha ha," Cy calls back. "Can't a girl get some privacy around here?"

Jay swivels back in front of the computer. He'll restart the game when Cy gets out so she can get the full experience, but for now, Jay can't wait. He's waited too long already.

****

```
<turn right into hallway
The front door slams shut, rattling the
windows. You hear crows calling in the
distance.

<open front door
You cannot open the front door. It's
been locked from the outside.

<turn right into hallway
You walk down the hallway. Piles of
filthy clothes slump against the walls.
You see a familiar jacket.

<look at jacket
This is your sister's jacket. She was
wearing it when she disappeared.

<pick up jacket
A cassette player falls from one of the
pockets.

<pick up cassette player
```

This belongs to your sister, too. She
never goes far without it.

<play cassette player

***

A garbled voice mumbles through the speakers, startling Jay so much he nearly falls out of his chair. Just as he turns up the volume and presses his ear to the foam, the voice goes quiet. He frowns at the speaker. This hasn't happened before. In the hundreds of playthroughs at Adam's house, this part never generated any sound. He's pretty sure the game didn't even have audio capabilities. Jay shakes his head. It's radio interference or something. He retypes the command with one hand, the other hovering near the volume dial.

The cassette player is empty.

"Okay…" Jay mutters. "Weird."

<take cassette player
Taken. You put the cassette player in
your pocket. Your sister will want it
back.

Cy's been awfully quiet for a while. Jay scoots his chair back for a second time. "Cy? You good?" No answer. Sighing, Jay gets up and pads down the hallway. "I'm at the puzzle now. Should I wait?"

Cy's shadow cuts the light at the bottom of the bathroom door. "You go right ahead and start, Jay."

Jay frowns. Her voice sounds a little odd. Strained. "Everything okay?"

"Just some tummy trouble. It's nothing."

Jay scrunches his face. "Gross. You need water or something?"

The shadow moves away from the door. "I'm fine, Jay."

As he stares at the light on his socks, the back of his neck pebbles with goosebumps. He rubs them smooth. The temperature in the apartment has suddenly dropped. That happens at night. No biggie. Jay retreats. He turns the heat up a notch on his way back to the computer.

***

```
<keep walking down the hallway
You continue walking down the hallway.
There are two doors. One is on your
right, the other on your left.

<open the door on the left
The door is locked.

<open the door on the right
You open the door. It's a bathroom.

<enter bathroom
```

```
You step inside the bathroom. The tub
is filled with brown, stinking water.
The walls are furry with mold. The
mirror has a crack down the middle.

<drain the tub
You reach into the brown water and pull
the plug. The water flows down the
drain and leaves streaks all over the
cracked porcelain. They look like
words.

<read the words
Mother of blood, mother of wounds. She
chopped off my head and she'll chop
yours off, too.

<look in the mirror
You look in the mirror and see a rat
scamper into the hallway. The door on
the left swings open.
```

***

Jay remembers this part. To progress down the game's normal path, he would go into the newly opened room to solve a puzzle with light switches. Two more puzzles would follow before the game ended with a disappointing thud. According to the forum guy's post, the alternative ending requires a different course of action. You need the rat. You need blood.

***

<Stomp on the rat's tail
You run into the hall and stomp on the
rat's tail before it vanishes into a
hole in the wall.

<pick up rat
You pick up the rat. Its frantic
heartbeat pulses against your hand.

<squeeze rat
The rat squeaks as you pop its organs.
Blood runs from its eyes.

<open bathroom cabinet
You open the bathroom cabinet and find
a dirty glass jar.

<take the jar
Taken.

<collect rat's blood in jar
You hold the rat over the jar. A half-
inch of blood collects at the bottom of
the glass.

<drink the blood
You shouldn't drink the blood.

<drink the blood
This is your last warning. You
shouldn't drink the blood.

<drink the blood
You drink the blood.

***

Jay waits, his breath gathering in his chest. Those were the only instructions the guy wrote. The cursor blinks on the screen like a winking eye. Nothing.

"Dang it," Jay whispers.

He leans back and rubs his face. The joke about the computer cost wasn't really a joke. Four months of rent, up in smoke. Cy is going to be livid. And their parents? Jay doesn't want to think about it, but he knows he's going to need their help. Again. He can hear his dad's lecture now.

Jay, you're 35 years old, when are you going to grow up? Jay, when are you going to stop messing around and get a real job? Jay, seriously, this is the last time your mother and I bail you out.

He collects himself after a few seconds. Yes, he made a dumb decision, but he should at least keep trying to crack the ending, right? It won't get his money back, but it would be ridiculous to get this far and just quit. Maybe he needs to solve the light switch puzzle, too.

***

```
<leave the bathroom
You leave the bathroom. Instead of
clothes, the hallway is now filled with
bodies. Their heads have been chopped
off.
```

"Yes!" Jay pumps the air with his fist, euphoria shooting through his veins.

Adam called him crazy, but here's the proof. There is a secret ending. Jay had been right all along. "Cy!" he yells. "You seriously need to get out here and see this!"

Faint muttering filters down the hallway, but Jay is already back to the game. He hasn't even noticed the faint screen glow is now the only light in the apartment. The bathroom light, the kitchen light, even the lights on the oven and microwave. All off.

```
<look at the bodies
Some of the bodies are small and some
are tall. They are covered in blood and
smell like a slaughterhouse. One of the
bodies wears a familiar jacket.

<look at the body
The corpse clutches a blood-smeared
cassette tape.

<put the cassette tape in the cassette
player
You click the tape into your sister's
cassette player.

<play the cassette
```

"Jayson..."

The sound of his full name kicks Jay back to reality. It's dark. And cold. He's covered in so many goosebumps, his skin feels like it might pop off his bones. All interest in the game evaporates and he grabs the speaker, his heart pounding. The voice soaks his ears even as he yanks the power cord free. It's louder now and unmistakably real. "Mother of blood, mother of wounds…"

"Hey!" Jay squeals. "Stop!"

"She chopped off my head…"

"Shut up!"

White fuzz fills the monitor and screeches from the broken speakers. "And she'll chop yours off, too."

The screen goes black, drowning the room in darkness. Jay's still sitting in his chair, his fingernails nearly piercing the plastic leather of the armrests. Icy sweat stings his eyes. *Cy*, he thinks. *That's Cy's voice.*

He sprints down the hallway, almost tripping over his own legs. His fists pound the bathroom door. "Cy!" he yells.

Twisting the knob does nothing; it's locked. Thankfully, everything in the apartment is old. It only takes Jay a few seconds to smash the door with his shoulder.

***

You are standing in your apartment
bathroom. The mirror is cracked down
the middle. There's blood soaking the
tiles and towels you haven't washed in
a month.

<look for Cyprus
She's not in the bathroom anymore.

<look for Cyprus
She's not in the living room. You throw
couch cushions as if she might be
hiding beneath them.

<look for Cyprus
She's not in either of the bedrooms.
You throw her blankets to the floor,
catching the lamp on her nightstand and
knocking it over. She's not in the
closet. She's not under the bed.

<call the police
Static boils from the cordless phone.
You throw it across the room when it
starts reciting "Mother of blood,
mother of wounds." The voice singes the
tender skin of your ear.

<leave the apartment
The door is locked from the outside.
You rub the skin off your palms trying
to twist the knob open.

<yell for help
No one answers your screams. You're
alone. So alone.

<open a window
You're on the fifth floor, but you have
no other choice. You'll have to jump.
Before you can open the window, you
catch the reflection of someone
standing behind you. It looks like a
woman. Her hair hangs like seaweed on
either side of her face. She's holding
an axe.

MOTHER OF BLOOD
Copyright (c) 1980 Immolate
Interactive, Inc. All rights reserved.

"A METEOROLOGICAL HISTORY OF CRYSTAL CLOUD ELDENA"

D.A. Jobe

One year ago, on May 16th, at 10:32a.m., a weather "disturbance" was recorded outside Front Royal, Virginia that would go on to cause apocalyptic levels of destruction and loss of life across the state. The government and scientific community termed it a 1000-year storm, claiming the destruction was from clusters of F5 tornadoes. Storm chasers Marie Davey and Britt Morelli of Updraft Tours documented the phenomena over 83 harrowing minutes. Their posts and recordings, recovered and put in order here, establish an early timeline for the event, and provide incontrovertible proof that this wasn't just a freak storm.

**Warning: some material may be disturbing.*

Updraft@Updraft_tours

Stunning high altitude cloud formation moving into Front Royal, Warren County, VA. Intense rainbands and quarter size hail hitting our position. Trained spotter.

10:38 a.m. May 16 31M Views

Reader's Added Note

This video is fake. The cloud wall is oversaturated with color and too high in the atmosphere. At 00:18 and 00:22 there is AI-generated flicker, with flashes of empty space. Beware of amateur storm chasers posting hype videos and spreading misinformation.

[VIDEO REMOVED]

[Transcript of Britt Morelli's phone call to the national severe weather line, 10:52 a.m., May 16th]

This is Britt Morelli, Updraft Tours, AO621Z. Currently on State Route 55, heading east, just past [*indistinct shouting from a different voice*]. Just past Jamestown Road in Front Royal. We observed a…massive storm approaching two miles to the west. Immense cloud tower. [*inaudible from road noise*] — ricane force winds, and trees down. Five crew…we lost five from hail—

[AUDIO CUTS OUT]

[Recovered footage, 11:05 a.m., May 16th, originally posted to weather discussion board, Inclement, by InsideOutUmbrella]

"We're in trouble, my friends." The phone camera shakes as Britt Morelli films herself in an extreme close-up from the passenger seat of Updraft Tours' SUV. "All two of you who even watch this channel. And Mom." She looks away, blinks.

"We don't know if it hit Belmont." Morelli turns the camera on Marie Davey at the wheel, who glances in the rearview mirror with red-rimmed eyes. Both women wear black *Updraft Tours* t-shirts.

Morelli films a traffic-clogged intersection ahead through sweeps of the windshield wipers, traffic lights twisting in the wind, flashing yellow. Rain pelts the glass in wind-driven gusts. People dart between cars on foot, covering their heads. The dash clock reads 11:05 a.m., but the day has been plunged into semi-darkness.

"We gotta get clear of this mess. Find an elevated spot."

"I'm trying," Davey says.

Morelli swings the camera around, over Davey clenching her fingers on the steering wheel, to the truck's cracked back window. There's a minivan on the road behind them, shadows of a driver and passenger inside. Dark, rain-swollen clouds fill the sky, pulsing with an eerie sunset-red light.

"I've never seen weather like this." Morelli's words are hard to make out over rain hammering the truck's roof. "Look at that rotation."

The phone flies from Morelli's hand, landing face down on the floor. "Jesus," she shouts, fumbling for it. A horn blares.

"Sorry," Davey says. "I had to get off this road."

Morelli faces front again, and houses scroll by on a residential street out the window. "Guys, if you're in the path of this thing, you need to take cover *now*. Don't mess around. Please share this."

She exhales, looks into the phone camera. "This morning, Leo saw there was something brewing over the Blue Ridge, so the whole crew went out to Eldena Hill to film and test the instruments. We got slammed by a huge wind gust. Marie and I were still in the truck. I thought a car ran into us. Outside it was a total gray-out, little bits of…silt in the air. Bigger pieces. Sharp, crystalized stuff." Her brow knits. "I thought we were in a tornado debris cloud. I really thought this is it."

Sirens sound in the distance and she glances behind her before continuing: "Marie and I got down on the floor behind the front seats. It lasted…maybe two minutes? The pressure was so intense." A pained look crosses her face. "As soon as it was over we ran out to find Leo and the others."

"Oh God." Davey moans off camera. "Oh God."

"Hey." The phone wobbles as Morelli turns to comfort Davey. "Marie? Hey—"

[*Video cuts out, immediately resumes with footage of emergency vehicles going the other way past the Updraft Tours truck on a two-lane hilly road.*]

Behind the wheel, Davey shows little emotion, but her cheeks are blotchy and tear-streaked. The women are stuck in another backup, light rain keeping the wipers in motion.

"Can you check the radar again?" Davey says.

"Yeah, hold on." Morelli puts the phone down face up on her lap, sucks in a sharp breath. "I must have really banged my shoulder back there." She examines her sleeve, brushes at it. Grabs her phone again, and after some jostling, hovers the lens over a live radar display on Davey's phone screen.

"Looks like the heavy stuff is a few miles back. After that"—she swipes the screen with a thumb, frowns—"white screen to Strasburg. Service must be down." She opens another radar app and it's the same. "Let's find an overpass or somewhere higher up for better service. We need to get eyes on that monster if it's still out there."

Morelli films their truck's slow progress. The road is bordered by swaying pine trees. The rain picks up. The glass fogs. Davey lowers her window a crack, cranks up the defrost. The sky gets cloudier, darker. The rain falls harder.

"Are these the outer bands?" Davey says, switching the wipers to high. "It started as just regular rain, didn't it?"

Both phones go off with an ear-splitting alarm.

[VIDEO CUTS OUT]

[Video clip posted to Updraft Tours' social media by Britt Morelli, 11:10 a.m., May 16th, unknown location]

The storm rises over the Blue Ridge Mountains like a dark, gaseous moon. Everything below and to the west, including the town of Front Royal, is obscured by thick, churning cloud cover. Lightning forks through the sky.

Morelli shouts over the howling wind. "Are you seeing this?"

The camera zooms in on a towering cloud wall within the supercell the color of ancient glacial ice, shot with veins of unearthly red. Not clouds exactly. Dark, marble towers in the *shape* of clouds. Immense walls of compacted, lethal debris. Rising to the upper reaches of the atmosphere.

"*Insane* motion!" Davey says off-camera. "Are there multiple funnel clouds in there or just one massive one?"

Morelli pans the camera shakily, strands of hair blowing over the lens. "Freaking *terrifying*," she says. "But beautiful."

She clears rain on the lens with her shirt. "I can't tell if it's because we're too far away, or something's wrong with the camera, but it keeps wanting to skip over sections of the storm, like it can't see all of it." The camera lowers as if she is taking it in with her own eyes.

"Britt," Davey says. "The wind's really picking up."

"Are those red sprites? *Impossible.*" She tries to capture the spectacle in a close-up, but only gets a grainy, orange-red smear.

"Britt!"

"Okay, okay. We can go." She sounds out of breath.

As Morelli slowly jogs to the truck, the camera jostles and picks up fragmented distant shots of funneling winds. The storm sparkles with an alien kaleidoscopic light that pixelates on film, the phenomena too complex for camera lenses to discern.

The footage causes migraines if watched for too long.

[Recovered footage, 11:22 a.m., May 16th, originally posted to weather discussion board, Inclement, by InsideOutUmbrella]

The video recording shakes as Morelli attaches her phone to a stand on the dash for a wide-angled view of the truck's cab. Her flushed face fills the frame before she slumps back in her seat.

"You okay?" Davey asks, scanning the rearview mirror. Visible through the windows, cars inch forward going the same direction on both sides of a two-lane road, stretching for miles behind them. "Maybe we should pull off somewhere."

"I want to get more footage when we get to Linden." The words are slurred, prompting a worried look from Davey.

"I think we have enough. Seriously, Britt. We need to go."

"We're fine." Morelli straightens with a grimace, favoring her left side. Her upper arm is red and bloody with what looks like road rash. Bits of shiny stuff embedded in her skin. "Just keep driving. We need to stay on it. This is *our* storm."

"Damn it," Davey mutters. She flicks her eyes to the mirror again, rocks forward in her seat as if it will make the cars ahead of them move faster.

"I just really think—" she starts, but there's nervous movement inside the car behind them, the driver twisting around, looking at the road. No. *Up.* And even though Davey hasn't looked herself, her shoulders stiffen as if she *feels* it. A gathering, swelling tension. Rolling from car to car to car.

"It's here," Morelli confirms, eyes to the side mirror. With effort, she detaches her phone from the stand. The footage judders and spins, catching sections of the truck's ceiling, the back seat strewn with empty and overturned equipment bins, wet pavement as she positions the device out the open window. Rain glazes the lens. A mountainous wall of clouds the color of dirty ice looms behind them. The storm sparkles with glass-like particles streaked with an iridescent, smoldering red.

It is the whole sky

On screen the image skips and cuts out, like there are elements of the storm the camera cannot capture, and so there is nothing in those spots but blank emptiness. The recording hums with a low, subsurface vibration, as if there is a tuning fork deep inside the camera that someone has tapped.

The vehicles surrounding *Updraft*'s SUV begin to crowd and crawl forward. A four-wheel drive peels off and bounces on the narrow shoulder at full speed, zooming through the grass, clipping another car's side mirror. Vehicles cut sharply out of traffic, crash into the sloping roadside.

"Hold on!" Davey shouts, and Morelli brings the camera back inside, closes the window and wipes the lens on her pants. She continues to film as Davey yanks the wheel when space opens up, gunning the engine. They rattle over the edge of the road into the grass and churned-up mud from the rain.

"Come on, come on," Davey repeats to herself, the car jouncing up and down. With all the cars flooding the shoulder, two narrow lanes have become three. The other shoulder drops sharply down a forested hillside; no escape there. It's chaos—abrupt stop-and-go.

"Watch it!" Morelli shouts, and Davey barely avoids a car in front of them. Traffic comes to a dead stop, exhaust clouds blowing in the torrential rain.

Davey looks at the camera with eyes too big for their sockets. *What do we do?*

Up ahead, a man steps out of his car as the rain intensifies. Horns blare. As the windshield wipers snap back and forth, Morelli videos him shouting and gesturing at the driver behind him.

"What the hell are you doing?" she mutters behind the camera. "Get back in the car."

Both women flinch when an object hits the windshield with enough force to cause a tiny crack. Another bounces off the hood of their truck. Morelli's camera zooms in on a jagged, pebble-sized piece of ice with a faint glowing red core inside.

"What *is* that?" Davey says.

Wind howls around the windows through the weather stripping, making an eerie whining sound. And now the sky opens, strafing the truck with sideways rain and hail, bits of debris, fine sharp sand. Paint fans off the car beside them, and the man who'd been standing a moment before, is thrown back against his car. The camera continues to film as his flesh is sand-blasted from his face into a fine pink mist carried off by the wind.
[VIDEO ENDS]

[Recovered footage from Marie Davey's phone, 11:30 a.m., May 16th, location unknown but believed to be near Linden, VA]

"I have to get Britt to a hospital," Davey says into the camera, standing beside the truck on the side of the road. She wipes her eyes, glances up at the leaden sky. Cars rush past, blowing her hair. "She says she's fine. But something's wrong. She keeps asking for water, keeps begging me to film. 'We have to document everything, Marie.'" Davey speaks in a level, forceful voice, mimicking her partner. "'It's *our* storm.'"

She rubs her eyes. Switches the camera view around to show the storm on the horizon as she walks to the back of the truck, the sound of gravel underfoot. Now, late afternoon, the sky has an unnaturally greenish-red cast, the massive wall of cloud sending out chemtrails of debris into the air like sideways tornadoes.

"I keep waiting for the damn thing to dissipate, but it just keeps getting stronger. The wind bands extend for miles. A bad one caught us on the road back there. I've never seen hail glow like that."

Standing there filming the storm, Davey falls quiet. "It's like Jupiter's red spot here on earth."

She lifts the cargo door, holds her fingertips in front of the camera lens. They are coated with glimmering, gemstone-colored flakes. "This stuff is all over the truck."

Road noise drowns out her voice as a convoy of emergency vehicles passes at fearsome speed. "Wait!" Davey rushes to wave them down. "Stop!" But they race by, sirens off.

The first responders are running away now.

[Traffic camera footage, 11:33 a.m., May 16th, Exit 13, Linden, I-66, posted on YouTube]

An elevated traffic camera, its lens fogged with moisture, points at a stretch of wet rural highway, a bridge overpass with a steady stream of vehicles racing to the east. The image flashes, a barrage of lightning creating a strobe effect. A swooping mass darkens the top of the frame like a storm cloud, but it is birds. Tens of thousands of them. Pigeons, crows, songbirds. They bank and wheel, scatter and dive, their bodies reflecting the light in ashy hues, silver to black to silver. Some dart for the overpass.

A yellow highlight circle appears on screen, tracking an SUV as it races toward the overpass, *Updraft Tours'* logo barely visible on its side. A dense cloud of glittery precipitation billows behind, cars vanishing into it, but not before they flatten back to front, as if stomped by a colossus.
[CAMERA SHAKES AND GOES DARK]

[Recovered footage from Marie Davey's phone, 11:40 a.m., May 16th, Linden/ I-66 overpass]

Davey adjusts the camera on the dash stand to point at her behind the wheel.

"Is it on?" Morelli says off camera. Her voice is oddly guttural. Wet.

"Yes." Davey wipes her face with her sleeve.

"We have to warn people."

A wind band hits them without warning, a gust so strong it picks up the rear of the truck and slams it down again. Davey holds on tight to keep from fishtailing. She floors the accelerator. The cab dims as she steers them under a bridge overpass and pulls over. She rests her forehead on the wheel. A sob catches in her throat.

The storm bears down, concrete cracking under the torrent. The car shakes. Dust sprinkles down from the overpass above.

The car jolts violently and Davey covers her head, as if expecting the overpass to collapse on them, but when the truck starts to creep forward, realization crosses her face. A vehicle behind them is pushing theirs, closer and closer to the shielding edge of the overpass.

"No! Stop!" She waves frantically through the back window at the ashen-faced driver, but he looks straight through her.

Davey yanks up on the emergency brake. Stands with all her weight on the brake pedal. But now the car behind her is being pushed too, as others force their way under the overpass. The air fills with the sound of crashing metal, horn blasts, screams, and flying debris. Davey wrenches the emergency brake until her arm muscles quiver, but the tires slide forward on the pavement. The truck inches forward until the hood is exposed to the open air. Instantly it crumbles under the onslaught of crystalized rain. The windows crack and spiderweb.

Davey releases her seatbelt and leans out of frame, presumably to help Morelli with hers. She shouts something indistinct. The truck is knocked violently from behind, and the camera jiggles. Britt Morelli's face appears for so brief a time it's easy to miss in the erratic shaking of the footage. Her face is blistered, crusted with caramelized blood, skin and tissue separated, sliding from the bone, as if boiled from the inside out. The flesh of her bare arms has softened and jellied, melding her body to her seat. It is unclear how she can still be alive. But her eyes are fever-bright, alert. Her blackened lips move as if she is trying to form words.

Another crash from behind sends a shockwave through the truck, knocking the camera off the stand. From the floor, it films Davey frantically trying the door handle a dozen times before realizing she has to unlock it first.

With a last, desperate look at Morelli, she grabs her phone before escaping out the driver's door.
[FOOTAGE CUTS ABRUPTLY]

[Recovered footage from Marie Davey's phone, 11:55 a.m., May 16th, Linden/ I-66 overpass]

The camera bounces as Davey climbs up the underside of the overpass, stumbling over a slope of large, smooth rocks. Others huddle there: a family with two kids, an older couple, a teen boy, their faces frozen in a rictus of fear. The force of debris hitting the structure overhead makes it sound like they are in a giant rock tumbler machine. Climbing as far as she can, Davey crouches with her arms over her head, the camera capturing flashes of cars crowded below the overpass, birds huddling together on a concrete shelf, and outside of the safety of the bridge overhang, fragments of twisted metal. The steel beams above tremble.

The downpour seems to go on forever, crystalized pellets or glowing ice—it's unclear which—clang off the pitted pavement and exposed cars. At last, the phone mic picks up quiet sobbing from people around her. The sky beyond the roof of the overpass lightens slightly. The storm bands pass.

People begin to stir and Davey stands up on shaky legs to make her way down the slope. *Updraft Tours'* SUV is a compacted heap of scored metal.

The camera picks up the chaos as drivers are swarmed by people, dragged from their vehicles before they can ram their way out. Screams and curses echo under the overpass.

Davey turns at the sound of a voice calling. A minivan waits with the side door open. A woman who'd taken shelter beside her on the slope waves. "Over here!"

Marie runs, climbs into the vehicle. Hands reach for hers. The van is packed, kids sitting on parents' laps. An alarm beeps as it drives off before the door can close all the way. Nobody speaks.

Squeezed in the back seat, Marie holds the phone camera up to the window until the overpass fades from view. "I'll stay with it," she whispers.

The minivan weaves around broken cars on I-66. Rain taps the window.
[VIDEO CUTS OFF]

⚠ EMERGENCY ALERTS   SUN 12/8 8:45 a.m.

"NUISANCE NOTIFICATIONS"

Amanda M. Blake

⚠ EMERGENCY ALERTS   SUN 12/8 8:47 a.m.

AMBER Alert: Child abduction in Frisco, TX. White Ford F150, Lic. CND 184. Victims are Luis (9) and Nina Morales (7), taken from home. Both were last seen wearing Marvel t-shirts. Suspect is Caleb Long (27), white, brown hair. Call 9-1-1 with information.

⚠ EMERGENCY ALERTS   SUN 12/8 8:53 a.m.

AMBER Alert: Child abduction in McKinney, TX. White Ford Maverick, Lic. unknown. Victim is Samira Rashanravan, age 5, taken from playground near home, last wearing pink jacket and purple sneakers. Suspect unknown, white male with brown hair, gray hoodie, tattoo of Ghost Rider on forearm, large birthmark on neck. Call 9-1-1 with information.

⚠ PUBLIC SAFETY ALERT   SUN, 12/8 9:13 a.m.

BLUE ALERT: LAW ENFORCEMENT OFFICER KILLED IN DALLAS, TX. VANITY PLATES DNT TRD, RED CHEVROLET SILVERADO 1500. LAST SEEN HEADING N ON 35E.

BREAKING NEWS   SUN, 12/8 9:30 a.m.

Officer Brian Smith shot in head. Police pursue suspect Les Miller, who allegedly abducted 7-year-old child. <u>For more...</u>

⚠ EMERGENCY ALERTS   SUN 12/8 9:35 a.m.

AMBER Alert: Child abduction in Dallas, TX. Red Chevy Silverado 1500, Lic. DNT TRD. Victim is blonde white female Dori Lilovich (7), snatched from sidewalk. Suspect is Les Miller (28), white male, brown hair, last seen wearing all black. Considered armed and dangerous. Call 9-1-1 with information.

⚠ EMERGENCY ALERTS   SUN 12/8 9:53 a.m.

AMBER Alert: Child abduction in Melissa, TX. Red Ford F150, Lic. WRW 923. Victim is Conner Friend (6), taken from Dollar General, last seen wearing a red cape and pajama pants. Suspect is white male Michael Concord (25), last seen wearing a black jacket and black shoes. Call 9-1-1 with information.

<u>Sunday, December 8: Texts from Janet Moore:</u>

10:07 a.m.

> Omg have you been getting all these Amber alert notifications?

10:07 a.m.

> Mom is telling me that it's those damn Democrats stealing children for their child trafficking ring in retaliation.

10:08 a.m.

> Only a matter of time bf Fox News and Newsmax pick it up.

10:09 a.m.

> God help us.

10:09 a.m.

> God help me.

⚠ EMERGENCY ALERTS   SUN 12/8 10:13 a.m.

AMBER Alert: Child abduction in Plano, TX. Black Dodge Ram with Q-Anon stickers covering rear windshield and back bumper, Don't Tread On Me yellow flag, vanity plate SCKTLBS. Victims are Carla (4) and Mira Gomez (3), brunette, Hispanic, taken from their home. Suspect is Conner Overstreet (33), white, light brown hair, six feet. Considered armed and dangerous. Call 9-1-1 with information.

<u>Sunday, December 8: Texts from Janet Moore:</u>

10:20 a.m.

> Told Mom that most of these guys seem like MAGA fanatics. Seriously, DNT TRD and the stickers and flag?

10:21 a.m.

> She said it's misdirection.

10:22 a.m.

> They're crisis actors now

10:22 a.m.

> Is matricide illegal?

> ⚠ EMERGENCY ALERTS   SUN 12/8 10:25 a.m.
>
> AMBER Alert: Child abduction in Richardson, TX. White Ford F350. Lic. unknown. Victims are Marlon Brady (7) and May Hatch (7), taken from park near home. White male suspect, brown hair, is unknown and at large, last seen in a black hoodie and white face mask. Call 9-1-1 with information.

> BREAKING NEWS   SUN, 12/8 10:30 a.m.
>
> Local police in NTX suburbs warns of multiple child abductions, unknown whether cases related. Chief recommends vigilance "until we figure out what's going on." For more...

Sunday, December 8: Texts from Marjorie Moore

10:35 a.m.

WATCH THE KIDS!!! THEY'RE COMING THEY'RE TAKING EVERYTHING WE HOLD DEAREST. DEMS HAVE FINALLY LOST THEIR EVER-LOVING MINDS.

10:37 a.m.

THEY'RE ANGRY WE WON. THEY'RE GOING TO TRAFFIC OUR CHILDREN AND GROOM THEM INTO SAME SEX SLAVES THAT VOTE BLUE WHEN THEY'RE TOO OLD TO USE ANYMORE

10:38 a.m.

JANET IS TAKING ME TO THE GROCERY STORE. DO YOU NEED ANYTHING?

10:39 a.m.

I'M GETTING YOU TOILET PAPER, SOUP, AND CRACKERS. WE NEED TO STOCK UP. FIRST OUR CHILDREN THEN THE LOOTING YOU'LL SEE.

10:40 a.m.

Janet told me to turn off the caps-lock to stop yelling at you. Love you. Mom.

⚠ EMERGENCY ALERTS   SUN 12/8 10:54 a.m.

AMBER Alert: Child abduction in Allen, TX. Red Chevy Silverado 1500, Lic. DNT TRD. Victim is black male Tate McNamara (6), taken from sidewalk. Last seen wearing a brown and green jacket. Suspect is Les Miller (28), also suspected of abducting Dori Lilovich (7) and shooting Officer Brian Smith. Do not engage. Suspect is considered armed and dangerous. Call 9-1-1 with information.

> ⚠ EMERGENCY ALERTS   SUN 12/8 11:03 a.m.
>
> AMBER Alert: Child abduction in Plano, TX. Green Jeep Wrangler with LOCK HIM UP on back tire cover, Lic. unknown. Victims are Vale Merriweather (3), Meredith Conners (3), and Lisa Malory (3), taken from Sunday school program at Custer Road UMC. Male suspect is unknown but violent, five volunteers hurt, two in critical condition. Call 9-1-1 with information.

Sunday, December 8: Texts from Janet Moore

11:05 a.m.:

Wtf is going on?

11:05 a.m.:

Mom is losing her shit, but so is everyone else?

11:07 a.m.:

My phone is blowing up, and so is my mind.

11:08 a.m.:

Mom keeps saying that the last guy was lib, so clearly this is a lib conspiracy.

11:09 a.m.:

> I asked her why the conservative kidnappers are crisis actors, but the liberal kidnapper is the real deal.

11:10 a.m.:

> I have now been disowned.

11:11 a.m.:

> Not really ha ha

11:12 a.m.:

> No joking now do you know where your kids are?

11:12 a.m.:

> And if this isn't political, what is going on? Child sacrifice to Satan?

BREAKING NEWS   SUN, 12/8 11:30 a.m.

ACTIVE SHOOTER: Alleged kidnapper/murderer Les Miller opens fire at Watter's Creek in Allen, TX, 3 miles from 2023 mass shooting at Allen Premium Outlets. Motive for Miller still unknown. Police warn for those in area to take cover. For more…

⚠ PUBLIC SAFETY ALERT   SUN, 12/8 11.35 a.m.

BLUE ALERT: OFFICERS TI MANN AND MATTEO ORTIZ KILLED DURING SHOOTING AT WATTER'S CREEK, ALLEN, TX. SHOOTER ALLEGED TO BE LES MILLER, SUSPECTED OF KIDNAPPING AND THE MURDER OF DALLAS OFFICER BRIAN SMITH EARLIER TODAY. SHOOTING STILL ACTIVE. CALL 9-1-1 WITH INFORMATION.

BREAKING NEWS   SUN, 12/8 11:45 a.m.

ACTIVE SHOOTER: Alleged kidnapper/murderer Les Miller opened fire at Watter's Creek, Allen, TX. Suspect still at large after killing first responders, abducting 2 siblings under 5 years old. Citizens encouraged to shelter in place. <u>For more...</u>

⚠ EMERGENCY ALERTS   SUN 12/8 11:59 a.m.

AMBER Alert: Child abduction in Allen, TX. Red Chevy Silverado 1500, Lic. DNT TRD. Victims are Missy (2) and Paulie Marano (4), dark brown hair, taken from lawn outside Frogg Coffee Bar and Creperie. Suspect is Les Miller (28), white male, brown hair, wearing all black. Considered armed and dangerous. Call 9-1-1 with information.

Sunday, December 8: Texts from Marjorie Moore:

12:05 p.m.:

I WANT TO SEE VIDEO OF THE KIDS RIGHT NOW

12:06 p.m.:

PROOF OF LIFE

12:06 p.m.:

LOVE YOU, MOM

BREAKING NEWS   SUN, 12/8 12:25 p.m.

Press conference with Dallas Police Chief: "Les Miller's Dallas home was set on fire ten minutes before we arrived with a warrant. Investigators found note fragments with statements like 'burn it all down' and 'things are not fine.' It is unclear whether Miller is linked to the other abductions." For more...

BREAKING NEWS   SUN, 12/8 12:45 p.m.

Search is still on for alleged abductor and mass spree killer Les Miller, who committed arson at his Dallas home but was last seen in Allen, TX. For more...

⚠ EMERGENCY ALERTS   SUN 12/8 12:55 p.m.

AMBER Alert: Child abduction in McKinney, TX. White Toyota Tundra, Lic. CND 098. Victims are Ivy (5), Paul (6), and Maisie Adamcyzk (8), taken from their home. Suspect is victims' father, Karl Adamczyk (36), white, blond. Last seen headed W on Sam Rayburn. Call 9-1-1 with information.

BREAKING NEWS   SUN, 12/8 1:13 p.m.

Child abduction epidemic: Alleged murderer/kidnapper Les Miller may be connected to a cluster of child abductions by other suspects in north DFW. Dallas Police Chief suggests shelter in place for those at home and lockdown on extracurricular programs.

BREAKING NEWS   SUN, 12/8 1:25 p.m.

Distraught mother of abducted Adamczyk children says husband Karl claims "humanity has no future" and "only sacrifice can correct the imbalance," cites multiple mental health issues. <u>For more...</u>

BREAKING NEWS   SUN, 12/8 1:35 p.m.

Dallas Police Chief states "no known motive for the abductions or murders, but given varied affiliations, they are not thought to be politically motivated." Les Miller and other alleged abductors still at large. For more...

BREAKING NEWS   SUN, 12/8 2:05 p.m.

Dallas Police Chief neither confirms nor denies that Caleb Long possessed a manifesto that advocates for an "act of depravity" to reset the world, warns against hysteria. For more...

BREAKING NEWS   SUN, 12/8 2:10 p.m.

Families of alleged child abductors claim suspects were "loving and sympathetic men" troubled by a variety of recent events; friend groups had become more "secretive." Police are working to get group text records for all suspects. For more...

<u>Sunday, December 8: Texts from Janet Moore:</u>

2:13 p.m.:

> I had to take Mom home and put one of her sedatives in the soup.

2:14 p.m.:

> Considered taking one myself. Compromised with wine.

2:15 p.m.:

> Have you heard from Mark yet?

2:16 p.m.:

> I'm sure the kids are fine.

⚠ EMERGENCY ALERTS   SUN 12/8 2:35 p.m.

AMBER Alert: Child abduction in Allen, TX. Blue Dodge Charger, Lic. WFR 109. Victims are Odette (5) and Lor Canales (6), taken from their own home. Suspect is the victims' father, Mark Canales (31), Hispanic, brown hair, last seen wearing a gray jacket and jeans. Call 9-1-1 with information.

<u>Sunday, December 8: Texts from Marjorie Moore:</u>

2:36 p.m.:

THEY'VE INFILTRATED OUR OWN HOMES THIS IS WHAT YOUR SICK LIB VALUES GET YOU. I TOLD YOU THAT MAN WAS NO GOOD NOW HE'S TAKEN MY GRANDBABIES I BLAME YOU I HATE YOU I HOPE YOU DIE SO YOUR KIDS CAN COME LIVE WITH JANET WELL PROTECT THEM BETTER THAN ANYTHING YOU DID I TOLD YOU NOT TO

2:40 p.m.:

WHO KNOWS WHAT YOUR PERVERT HUSBAND IS DOING TO THEM WHAT HES BEEN DOING TO THEM FOR YEARS HOW COULD YOU NOT KNOW GODDAMN YOU SARA

2:45 p.m.:

YOUR NEVER GOING TO SEE YOUR KIDS AGAIN

2:46 p.m.:

CHURNING IN THE MACHINE

2:47 p.m.:

THE END ISN'T NIGH ITS HERE

2:48 p.m.:

HOW COULD YOU LET THIS HAPPEN? HOW COULD YOU WAIT SO LONG BEFORE REPORTING THEM MISSING? THEY'RE PROBABLY ALREADY DEAD AND EATEN

2:50 p.m.:

This is Janet. I took Mom's phone away. I'm so sorry about this. I thought for sure she was asleep. She's just upset. She doesn't mean any of it.

BREAKING NEWS　　　　　SUN, 12/8 3.15 p.m.

Dallas PD and surrounding stations urge citizens to provide concrete confirmation for sightings and to exhaust all possibilities before calling in missing children. Dispatch is inundated; AMBER Alert system "is not efficient for mass abductions." <u>For more...</u>

<u>Sunday, December 8: Texts from Mark Canales:</u>

3:35 p.m.:

I'm sorry I couldn't tell you about this

3:36 p.m.:

You wouldn't understand

3:37 p.m.:

> The world is falling apart. Society is crumbling but held together by thicker and thicker funnel spider web. The spider bites, injects its venom. The spider feeds upon us. We can't keep going like this. People aren't willing to do what must be done. We're afraid. We tell ourselves we're building a future. There is no future if things continue on like this.

3:39 p.m.:

> No one wants to make an uncomfortable sacrifice. So the only answer is an excruciating one.

3:42 p.m.:

> I don't want to do this. I have no choice.

3:43 p.m.:

> I know you'll never forgive me. I'm not asking for forgiveness. I know that this is the only way.

3:45 p.m.:
[picture attachment]

3:47 p.m.:

> Don't worry. They'll go peacefully.

> **BREAKING NEWS**   SUN, 12/8 3.50 p.m.
>
> Mass murder-suicide of abducted children and abductors discovered in Raytheon parking lot in Richardson, TX. Security guards shot. First officer at scene shuttled to hospital after alleged breakdown. <u>For more...</u>

<u>Sunday, December 8: Texts from Janet Moore:</u>

3:55 p.m.:

> I don't know what to do about Mom. She keeps shouting about hell, Revelation, the End Times, Obama, Trump, Biden, Epstein, Clinton... She doesn't even remember our current president. She's making less and less sense, and that wasn't exactly a prerequisite for her rants before. I don't know what to do.

3:57 p.m.:

> I hate to put this on you, but I'm scared.

4:00 p.m.:

> Omg I didn't read the latest notification. I'm so sorry Were Odette and Lor part of that are they dead?!

4:01 p.m.:

Oh my fucking god.

4:02 p.m.:

On our way

⚠ EMERGENCY ALERTS   SUN 12/8 4:20 p.m.

WEATHER ALERT: An unexpected storm system has developed over the DFW area, primarily the northern counties. System is still new but projections indicate potential for multiple lightning strikes and hail. The following counties have a SEVERE THUNDERSTORM WARNING until 10:00 p.m....

⚠ EMERGENCY ALERTS   SUN 12/8 4:30 p.m.

WEATHER ALERT: Hail confirmed in Collin and Dallas Counties, meteorologists say conditions appear perfect for tornadoes. The following counties have a TORNADO WATCH until 10:00 p.m....

> **BREAKING NEWS** SUN, 12/8 4.40 p.m.
>
> Mass abductions in major cities such as Dallas, Chicago, San Francisco have led to horrifying mass murder-suicides, suggesting coordinated effort. No word as to manifesto or suicide pact; no cult leader or terrorist organization has taken credit for these gruesome deaths. <u>For more...</u>

> ⚠ **EMERGENCY ALERTS** SUN 12/8 4:45 p.m.
>
> WEATHER ALERT: A tornado has been confirmed in your area. Take shelter immediately. TORNADO WARNING through 6:00 p.m. TORNADO WATCH through 10:00 p.m.

<u>Sunday, December 8: Texts from Janet Moore:</u>

5:03 p.m.:

> Rain is so bad we can hardly see. Had to pull over at a Shell after tornado notification. Are you okay?

5:05 p.m.:

> Bad question. Are you safe?

5:15 p.m.:

I just watched a tornado flip a dozen cars going down Alma, then another one take out a Cici's Pizza. What's going on here? And how is it so dark and green at the same time?

5:17 p.m.:

Mom is calling the tornadoes God's wrath. I'm afraid she's going to try to "meet her maker." No one's going to notice a Silver Alert on their phones in this mess.

5:19 p.m.:

I don't know what to do. Where do I go? They keep coming. There's no power here. Is there any where you are?

5:31 p.m.:

If we don't get there, I love you so much. Mom does too even if she's having an episode right now. I love you and I'm so sorry about everything

5:32 p.m.:

Really feels like the end of the world, doesn't it? Maybe she's not so wrong about that.

BREAKING NEWS   SUN, 12/8 6.31 p.m.

White House press secretary: Strange meteorological phenomena has "nothing to do with the mass murder-suicides." President scheduled to address the American people at 7 p.m.

Sunday, December 8, 6:36 p.m.

Low Battery
6% battery remaining
please charge or turn on

Power Saving Mode

"TO THE ATTENTION OF GERALDO"

by Chris Panatier

MEMO to REDACTED, Joint Chiefs
From NRO Staff
Re: Codename CENTRALIA REDUX
Date: January 8, 1988

Ten days ago, a subterranean proliferating anomaly was detected outside of Orrville, Ohio. You requested that National Reconnaissance conduct a records review for potentially correlative data. NRO staff has flagged a set of videos recently received from the CBS Broadcast Center (original shipping slip included). NRO staff believes that the attached excerpts are most relevant to your investigation of the CENTRALIA REDUX anomaly and advise that you view them without delay.

NRO

JVC Brand VHS Tape: "Rental Basement #1"

10/10/87
11:12 a.m.

A man's face fills the screen. It is round and bearded and knows whiskey. He's so close to the lens that the gin blossoms pixelate. An old scar travels down his forehead and onto his cheek.

"So, look," he says, adjusting the camera on its tripod while battering the microphone. "I'm down here in the rental house…" He tilts the camera to level the shot while glancing over his shoulder at a light blue wall that is largely blank, but for a vertical hole. "…And I figure hey, if they can do it on *This Old House*, then why can't old Ted Abernathy?" He plays with the focus, his face blurring briefly into a maroon sun on a dusky background before returning to clarity. He steps away from the camera with hands on hips, head tilted in a *that-oughta-do* kind of way.

"That oughta do. Anyway, so, see this wall back here? Just a few studs and drywall. There's space on the other side. Not unusual. Most of the houses on this block were slapped on top of big old basements that most folks didn't need. So whenever they got around to building 'em out, well, they didn't want to mess with angles and just roughed in the squares. Cheaper. Less work. But they lost square footage."

A toolbox sits on a folding chair. Ted lifts a can of Old Milwaukee from among the tools and tosses his head back for an indulgent swallow. "Ahhhh." He returns the can. "So anyways, I had thought I would knock this wall down, finish it out, and then maybe move over here myself. Then I could get Mom out of that piss-bin they call a retirement community. I could live downstairs here and put her up on the ground floor. Be there to take care of her. Maybe make up for losing my rosary necklace she gave me." He pauses for a long moment, then finishes the Old Milwaukee. "Still don't know how I lost it. No idea."

"But that isn't why I'm recording. I'm recording because *this*." He goes to the hole in the middle of the wall, reaches through it, and raps on something on the other side. It barely makes any noise. "That's metal. Rusty, but solid as hell. Not the furnace, either—that's back over there." He points behind the camera. "Seems big. Tough to judge the size." He squeezes his mouth and chin between thumb and fingers. "Could be one of those giant safes the mob used to use. They would have had to lower the thing in here and then build the house around it. Could be the Cosa Nostra put in this wall." He slaps it and laughs. "Remember last April when Geraldo opened Capone's safe? Talked for two whole hours and didn't find shit. My God.

"So, anyways, we'll video it and see what we find. If it's a safe and there's money, well then, I'll buy the house next door and me and ma can be neighbors." He picks up a sledgehammer. "Here goes."

Ted puts the sledge through the drywall. It smashes through so easily that the handle slips out of his hand and into the void behind. "Son-bitch!" He breaks away some of the drywall with his hands and leans inside to retrieve the tool.

He makes quick work of the wall, exposing a large, oxidized steel panel set a few feet off the ground. Nearly as tall as Ted, it is roughly square and bricked in on either side, creating a second wall behind the now-demolished sheetrock. Ted wipes his brow and turns to the camera. "Not sure I expected that. Don't know why you'd do brick and drywall. This, though," he says, tapping the head of the sledge on the metal, "this has got me wondering. There's no combo and no lock, so it isn't a safe. Not by manufacture, anyway. But that's a door, alright. There're hinges behind this stud." He backs away and takes a huge swing at the vertical two-by-four, breaking it in half, then wiggles the pieces out of the frame. "See?" He points to four sets of hinges running up the side. Walking to the other side, he says. "And this side's welded." He knocks on the steel. "Anybody home?" He chuckles as he approaches the camera to turn it off, and mutters, "Hope not."

10/10/87
5:14 p.m.
Ted wields a blue angle grinder. "Guy at the hardware place said it's either this or I need one of those specialized circular saws for steel with diamond blades, and I explained that Ted isn't made of cash. He did have a good piece of advice, though, I'll give him that. He said hit the hinges instead of attacking the weld. A lot less work for the grinder and the cutting discs."

He sips his beer and puts on sunglasses. "Safety first."

Sparks fly as the grinder bites the old steel of the first hinge. After ten minutes, he pauses. "Overheating." He nurses the beer and resumes cutting. After ten more minutes, he reports the disc is shot, he's got to replace it. "Only bought three of these."

10/10/87
7:24 p.m.
Ted is back from the hardware store with more cutting discs. He's cut through two of the four hinges.

JVC Brand VHS Tape: "Rental Basement #2"
10/10/87
10:01 p.m.
Ted whoops triumphantly as the grinder slices through the last bit of hinge. "Fuck yeah! That's how you do it!" He thrusts the grinder over his head like a trophy. Several more cans of Old Milwaukee litter the floor.

"Alright, well, work isn't done yet," he says, setting the grinder onto the floor and picking up a crowbar. "The hope is I can put enough leverage on this side to bend that weld over yon. I really don't want to have to get Trent down here with his cutting torch and have to split the money with him." He fits the crowbar into a notch and pulls back with a loud grunt. Straining, he grunts, "Fuckinshit!"

JVC Brand VHS Tape: "Rental Basement #2-6"
10/11-10/14/87
Ted makes numerous attempts to break open the door on the big steel panel. He even sledges out the brick on either side to look for alternative ways in, but reports that the box, which he says goes back about twelve feet, is solid all the way around. He is plainly intoxicated during most of this.

JVC Brand VHS Tape: "Rental Basement Lucky #7"
10/16/87
6:16 p.m.
Ted has constructed a makeshift scaffolding using two-by-fours. Set between the door and the camera, it nearly reaches the ceiling. The crowbar is wedged into the door where Ted made his cut. A cable runs from the end of the crowbar up over the top of the scaffolding, and down to a steel tray that Ted has loaded with weightlifting plates and bricks. He continues piling bricks onto the tray while cursing that the door has not budged. Eventually, the cable snaps and slingshots backward, ejecting the beer out of Ted's hand. The tray crashes down and he howls as the bricks smash his foot.

JVC Brand VHS Tape: "Rental Basement #8"
10/17/87
8:32 a.m.

Ted appears in overalls, an apron, gloves, and a welding helmet with the visor up. "Riddle: how does one get one's friend who has an acetylene cutting torch to loan it to you *and* give you a lesson? Answer: have in your possession the highly coveted Nintendo Entertainment System with the *Mario/Duck Hunt* Zapper pack with which to barter. Hell, I'll buy a new one if this old girl is loaded with cash." He taps the cutting nozzle on the metal box with a sharp *ping*.

10/17/87
9:41 a.m.

Ted is in front of the camera looking haggard. "Harder than it looks, but I've got that whole damned seam cut except for the last little bit." He gestures to the door on the box, sagging some under its own weight. "Geraldo: if you're out there, wish me luck."

Ted climbs a ladder set to the side of the box and leans over the top. A bright point of light washes out the screen as he cuts the final inches.

The massive door comes free and drops down in front of the box, exposing a strip of blackness across the top. Ted hoots and flips the helmet off his head, wheels the cutting apparatus to the side, pulls the ladder out of the way, and places himself before the camera. Excited, he smooths back his thinning hair.

"Let's flip this door down and see what we came for. Ted's Box. Theo-dora's Box. Get it?" Chuckling, he pulls off the gloves and exchanges them for a fresh can of Old Milwaukee from the toolbox, clinks it against the metal door and drinks it down. He places the empty on the ground out in front of the box, then pushes the panel over. It thunders to the floor in a cloud of dust.

Ted stares at the camera for a long moment, then turns to look inside the box, which appears as a well of black on the screen.

"Well, shit. Why the hell would you go through all the trouble of putting the goddamned thing here, weld it shut, and hide it behind a wall if you weren't gonna put anything inside?" Ted climbs in. It's big enough that he can stand with his head dipped forward.

He advances inside until his back is a smudge in the dark. His voice echoes out. "This thing goes way farther on the inside than it should. I'm a good twenty-five feet in and still can't see where it ends." He flicks his lighter and a distant flame appears deep in the black. "See?" The flame moves as Ted continues ahead. "Hey, whoa. What in the double-stuffed fuck?" The flame disappears and seconds later Ted shoots out of the box, almost tripping across the amputated door. He runs to the camera and shoves something up against the lens. It's a VHS tape.

His voice shakes. "Look. Look at that." He scans around the basement. "Somebody is fuckin' with me." He holds the tape to the camera so the label can be read and traces his dirty finger along the words while reading aloud. *"For whoever finds this, especially if it's you, Ted, you dumbass."* He pulls it back and stares at it. "That…is my fucking handwriting." He reaches for the camera. "I got to watch this."

JVC Brand VHS Tape: "For whoever finds this, especially if it's you, Ted, you dumbass"

2/12/87
11:19 p.m.

Ted's face appears. Thin, like it's been winnowed away. His eyes are bloodshot and the scar on his head is a fresh wound, just scabbed over. His jocular affect is gone. "God, I hope you're not watching this, Ted. Cause if you are, it means you weren't smart enough to see a door that didn't wanna be opened and fuckin' opened it anyway. It means you forgot the reason you closed in the first place.

"Here's what you're gonna do: You're gonna watch what I have to say, get the tape back to exactly this point, throw it *back* into the box, and weld it shut. Forever. Trent's got a rig, he'll loan it to you. That numbnut loves *Duck Hunt*, maybe y'all do a trade. Fuck, man. I knew I didn't hide this thing well enough. Should have bricked it all the way across, just didn't have time." Behind this strange Ted is the steel box with bricks laid to the ceiling on either side. "Too late now. Anyways, you're gonna weld it, and brick it up right this time. Then pretend you never found the box and never say shit.

"If you're watching this, it means you went inside, found the tape. That's the one and only time you go in. Never—I repeat—*never* again. When you put the tape back, you toss it the hell in there, got me?" Ted rubs his hands over his face. They look thin, almost skeletal.

"Okay, Ted. You have your instructions. Now for an explanation. This tape is at about the halfway point, I guess. Rewind it to the beginning and start there. Watch it all. Then do exactly as I said. That's it. Go, Ted."

2/10/87
9:14 p.m.

A much more well-fed Ted holds his face to the camera, blanching it in the spotlight, then flips it around. The inside of the steel box stretches out before him. "Recording for posterity," he says. "Just like old Geraldo. Looks like we both rolled snake eyes on potential riches, buddy. Anyways, wish me luck." He brings a rosary necklace to his lips, kisses it, and hustles ahead.

"These rental properties are full of surprises, but I've never seen anything like this. I don't even know what the hell's going on. Thought it was an old boiler at first, but it's humungous. There's no piping, no power. Not a vault, unfortunately. Or maybe it is. Makeshift perhaps. Either way, it's bereft of cash, as they say."

He stops and aims the camera backward. The entry to the box is a distant square. "Fuck me, man. How far does this go? I gotta be under the next-door neighbors' place by now. Probably past it." He continues ahead with the camera's light the only source of illumination.

Eventually, the smallest of pinholes appears like a single star in a black sky. Ted trots toward it, breathing hard. "Jesus, that must be five hundred feet away." The camera droops some as he moves faster. The pinhole becomes a growing square of light—the end of the box, which by now is clearly a tunnel.

The world on the other side comes into focus. Ted makes a confused and regretful noise. "No, nuh-uh. That's not possible." He turns and points the camera back in the direction he'd come to pure blackness, then again to the end of the tunnel and what is clearly his rental house basement, just as he left it.

He scurries to the metal edge of the box and slowly steps out. "Uh, hello?"

The chair is there, with his toolbox and a can of Old Milwaukee. His collapsed scaffolding and spilled bricks are there on the floor. He pans over the room. "You mighta got some bad 'shrooms, Ted."

He steps over and lifts the Old Milwaukee, wobbles it between fingers, then tips it over. What seems like watery blood pours out. Squealing, he drops it. The ground rumbles.

The camera goes with Ted as he checks the stairs. It angles to the door at the top. He clomps up the steps and turns the knob. It opens to the kitchen. He sucks in his breath.

The room is cast in orange light flowing in from the curtainless windows and back door. It is silent. He goes across the old tile and gazes outside. There is nothing beyond but a swirling void, as if the house is floating adrift in a dimensionless, glowing soup. He runs to the big bay window in the front room. There is no yard, no street—only what seems like the burning remnants of an exploded star. The structure quakes. Ted swallows loud enough for the mic to pick it up.

The camera drops to the side as Ted scrambles to the basement stairs and nearly throws himself down. He shoots across the floor and leaps into the box. The camera slips to the side and the light of the basement jiggles as it recedes.

Ted runs, striking his head repeatedly on the ceiling of the tunnel. Soon the basement is gone and the box, but for the camera's light, is enveloped in darkness.

He barrels forward, breath wheezing out of him, wondering aloud what he's just seen and where he's been. Then he makes a startled noise and shuffles to a stop, the last echoes of his footsteps continuing ahead.

The camera slowly rises and comes to focus on something in the tunnel. Pale. A body. Sitting against the side, legs out in front. Naked. Emaciated. It turns its head and smiles. A thin, but otherwise perfect copy of Ted. He says, "I've been waiting for you."

Ted swallows again.

"I know," says the man. "It must be surprising, finding me here. Now. But it means it's all working like it's supposed to. This is a good thing."

"Who…who are you?"

"I'm an evocation."

"What?"

"That which is evoked by the Span," he says. "I'm the new you, buddy."

"Why do you look like me?"

The evocation straightens against the side of the box. "I'm sorry to say this, but you can't return home."

"Fuck are you talking about?" Ted starts ahead. The naked man springs upright, animal quick, and assumes an aggressive stance in the middle of the tunnel. "You better step aside," says Ted.

"I can't do that," says the evocation. Orange light begins to fill the interior of his nose, mouth, and ears.

"Why not?"

"You were in the other place for too long. I can't let you cross."

"What was that back there? Hell?"

"The name doesn't matter. But yes. You traveled to one of its nodes."

"I was there for two minutes."

"Doesn't matter, Ted. You're demonflesh now."

"And what the fuck are you supposed to be?"

"Well, I'm your replacement. Untainted by damnation. Summoned by the Span to replace the you that crossed over. The Span must remain a secret."

"Span?"

"This." His pale arms gesture to the walls of the tunnel.

"What's the point of keeping it a secret if no one uses it?"

"I didn't say no one uses it, Ted."

Ted places the camera on the floor and steps out in front. "Move aside."

The evocation shakes his head. "I literally can't do that."

Ted pulls a screwdriver out of his pocket and wields it like a knife. "I got my mom to take care of." His voice shakes.

"I will care for her. I promise."

"The fuck you will."

"The Span must remain hidden."

Ted scoffs. "*You* know about it."

"Now, yes. But I won't remember it for too long once I'm back on your side and fully become you." The evocation tilts his head. "I promise your mother will be cared for. I have only one purpose: to keep hell from crossing over."

"Fuck that." Ted launches down the tunnel, slashing wildly with the screwdriver. It slices the man's face, but that is all Ted manages. The evocation moves insect-quick, breaking Ted's arms and legs at the joints. His shrieks abbreviate with the snapping of his neck.

The evocation crouches beside the body and hovers his hands above it. "Sorry, Ted." His fingers begin to extend, growing many feet in length. Tentacle-like, they go about undressing Ted's corpse. The evocation dons the clothing, then picks up the camera and runs the rest of the way to the rental house basement.

He secures the camera to the tripod. Behind him, the door to the box hangs open on its hinges. "Gotta get this thing welded shut before I forget what I'm doing and why I'm doing it." He finds a rag and presses it to the wound on his forehead. He reaches out and the screen goes black.

2/12/87
1:19 p.m.

The evocation, aka New Ted, finishes bricking in the sides of the box. Materials for framing and drywall lay stacked on the floor. Taking an Old Milwaukee from the toolbox, he approaches the camera. His face has filled out some.

Holding up the can, he says, "This stuff is truly terrible, Ted, but I confess I'm getting a taste for it." He takes a drink. "I've been to see your mom—our—my—mom. It's like nothing ever changed. I want you to know that. I'm exactly you. If you—which would be me—are dumb enough to open this door that I am going through so much trouble to close, don't freak out when you learn that the original us is dead. We love Ted's mom just as much as he did. And she loves us back." New Ted tosses the can over by the chair. "It's already getting fuzzy to me what's on the other side of that box, so I gotta get this done and we can forget it's there and leave it be for all time. You won't see any more videos from me. I'm saving the last bit of tape to record the instructions, which you should have already watched. Bye, Ted. Bye, uh, me."

JVC Brand VHS Tape: "Rental Basement #8"
10/17/87
10:23 p.m.

Ted appears on screen. The scar on his forehead is faded. His face is drawn. "So, there are two of me. *Were* two of me? Real me—" he looks back to the box, "dead in the tunnel—and fake me, evocation me, current me. Real me went to hell and tried to come back. But I…materialized…and killed him, then assumed his life and forgot what I really was. Apparently." He flicks the VHS. "All on tape."

He traces the scar. "I once thought I got this in a bar brawl. Guess I just invented that?" He holds up his hand and stares at his fingers. "What am I really, if I'm not original me?"

JVC Brand VHS Tape: "Rental Basement #9"
10/18/87
2:30 a.m.

Ted tosses over his toolbox in a rage. He slaps his neck. "I forgot to get the necklace off my own goddamned corpse!"

3:30 a.m.

Dejected, Ted sits on the floor beneath the box. Something that looks like his best attempt at a timeline is scrawled in chalk on a scrap of drywall. Eventually, he mutters, "So if this is all real, the original me is in there, dead. And with Mom's rosary still around my neck."

4:10 a.m.

Ted stops pacing, looks at the camera. "I gotta go get something."

JVC Brand VHS Tape: "Rental Basement #10"
10/18/87
7:11 a.m.

Ted stands framed by the black interior of the box, head hung, brow furrowed. Grimacing. He takes up a flashlight from the spilled tools, clicks it on and off a few times, then shoves it into a pocket. He lifts the back of his shirt. A pistol grip sticks up from his waistband. He pulls it out, lets it hang in his hand.

7:34 a.m.

He goes in.

8:18 a.m.

Gunshots.

8:25 a.m.

A naked man, spattered red, eyes wide with fear, emerges from the shadows and scrambles out of the box. His chest weeps from a constellation of holes. A few seconds later, Ted appears, bloodied and limping, one of his arms bent the wrong way. The first man spins and cries out. Ted fires. The man's head blooms open.

Grinning wildly, Ted approaches the camera and shoves the rosary up against the lens. "Look at that!"

A blast of air musses his hair. He turns to the box, its black throat now glowing hot. "Oh shit." He grabs the camera and drags it out of the basement. Cinders chase him up the stairs.

SHIPPING STATEMENT

DATE
December 26, 1987

RECIPIENT:
To the Attention of Geraldo
Rialto Theater/CBS Broadcast Center
1481 Broadway
New York, NY 10036

SENDER:
Not Provided

CONTENTS:
Eleven (11) VHS tapes

"TRAIL CAM 004"

Matthew J. Hockey

Three men sat packed into the baking hot video suite in the upstairs computer lab of St. Isidore, Montana police department. The first was Darryl Lusk, a short, bald and bullet-headed black detective with polarized shooting glasses tucked arm first into the unbuttoned collar of his oxblood polo shirt. The smell of freshly applied skin moisturizer hung heavy on him and he kept rubbing his thumbs across his fingers like they were still greasy. Joshua Jackson, his partner, and the one who had called this meeting, was twenty five years his senior, a cadaverous, hollow-cheeked white man who looked as though clouds of condensed cigarette ash would come wheezing out of his suit if you hit him hard enough with a snow shoe. He was nervous to begin too, by the looks of it; he kept tapping a fancy butane lighter in the shape of a bishop chess piece on the table edge, waiting to speak and coughing into a balled-up rag.

Their guest, Dr. Olson Boyd-Parry, professor of Ecology and Anthropology from Montana State U, was every inch the outdoorsman of his reputation, wearing waterproofs despite the unseasonal heat and busted air conditioning, home-cured leather Stetson balanced perfectly on one knee. His beard sat on his chin like an upside-down mountain, slopes of slate gray capped with veins of ice white, though the hairs on his beefy arms crossed over his gut were brown-black and thick as the pelt of some forest animal.

"What's this all about?" the doctor asked. "Your secretary didn't tell me too much before I came down here."

"Oh, Darlene. She's not our or anybody else's secretary," Detective Lusk said.

"That'd be Detective. First Class Wagner. She's not going to be here today on account she's taken some personal time." Here Detective Jackson got up and opened each of the small room's three tiny windows, contributing nothing but the scent of ponderosa pine and sulphur from the nearby hot spring. The dust from the gravel-aggregate works on the end of the block triggered his wet cough once more.

They lapsed again into awkward silence, quiet enough to hear the laughter and grab-assery of the motorcycle cops on the rank out front. The detectives shot each other a look, neither of them knowing how to begin now they'd got the doctor here. Boyd-Parry grabbed the initiative.

"Not to get too ahead of myself but I've a feeling, seeing as how we're in the video lab and not a hotbox, you've brought me in as an expert witness to something or other, and further I'd hazard it pertains to whatever it is happened to those poor folks out in the backcountry."

"Yeah. Something like that. Yeah," Lusk said.

"The Dunbars," Jackson said, finally realizing he was tapping the lighter and putting it away in his pocket.

Nobody in town had talked about anything else in the eight days since they were discovered. A family of four wiped out at their summer house out in the forest bordering on the national park. Aside from the obvious human tragedy of it, they were summer folks, incomers, here to enjoy the great outdoors. With them killed, and in such gruesome circumstances, plenty of the other campers and vacationers and day trippers had steered their RVs well clear of St. Isidore. Businesses relied on their trade. Hell, Jenny at the Kootenai Roadhouse had to let all her temp wait staff go early, cancel the battle of the bands. The camping plots were mostly empty and the people in those that were filled huddled together around their fires and hunting rifles. Only the sporting goods and gun stores were doing well, selling clean out of heavy grain brass head rifle rounds and boxes of double-ought buck. Local news was aflame with it, whipping people up, taking every opportunity to remind folk that whichever bear did it was still out there, roaming.

"That's why I wanna thank you for coming out here on such short notice. It's a long drive and you musta been busy up at the university," Lusk said.

"No lectures til the students pile back in September. You saved me from paper-grading is all."

Lusk carried on as if the doctor hadn't spoken, reading from an over-rehearsed script.

"Once you see what we have here you'll appreciate why we didn't e-mail it over."

"It gets pretty sporty in parts." Jackson leaned over the table, the tip of his tie dipping into a cup of stale coffee as he reached for the mouse. "Any time you want to tap out, give a holler. It's our job to see this kind of thing. No reason you should have to carry it around with you—"

"Detectives, I've walked every inch of this forest since I was a pup. I've seen things. Play your tape."

The video swelled to take over the whole screen. Sunset as seen from the deep woods, the camera was midway up the trunk of a pine overlooking a game trail covered in a carpet of dropped needles. An overlay at the top read: *Trail Cam 004*.

The focus snapped to movement in the lower right of the screen. A doe mule deer, not long since left its mother's teat, cropped at the fresh new buds on a sprawling bush. The sound of its chewing seemed very loud as the rest of the forest fell to silence. After a few more bites the doe seemed to realize something was wrong and froze, looking up, eyes wide. There was a crash off-camera, and the doe sprayed pellets of shit and bolted back the way it came, blowing alarm calls as it ran.

The camera jiggled up and down, bouncing against its strapping. The auto-focus darted around, treating everything as movement. Boom. Boom. Boom. Massive juddering footsteps ran toward the camera from behind. Then, with a deafening smash, the whole tree uprooted and the camera fell forward as a rain of soil, leaves and splintering roots fell around it.

Except the camera didn't fall the whole way. Whatever knocked the tree down scrabbled through the branches and the camera tangled around it somehow. Its breathing was right next to the mic, drowning all the other sounds with its whuff, whuff, whuff. It shook and shook, saliva flew in front of the lens but the camera stayed wedged tight against it. The creature gave up after a few moments and turned as smoothly as a compass needle vectoring back to magnetic north and, once it found its bearing, charged off at top speed.

It moved in an eerily straight line, not deviating in the slightest, powering through bushes and trees, sliding over rocks and through slippery mud, even when obvious paths looped around to either side of the rough terrain. Its breathing never changed, just that same strangled huffing as though trying to breathe through a damaged throat. Whuff. Whuff. Whuff.

It barreled through a line of decorative bamboo marking the edge of a property and out the other side onto a winding driveway. Automatic lights flashed on and the camera paused for just long enough to read the words carved into a decorative stone at the side of the path: "Welcome to the Dunbar's."

It rounded the next corner and there was the house. A three-story log pile cabin with a wraparound deck. A million dollars' worth of summer home, lit up with spotlights so it could be seen clear across the valley.

A brand-new Mercedes Benz G class luxury SUV was pulled right up to the front steps. The creature slowed as it approach, its breathing fluttering out into one long whoosh like wind rising through trees.

The father of the family, Wayne Jay Dunbar, mining company exec, was unloading supplies from the back of the SUV, looked like for a cookout with everybody he knew invited. Sacks of ribs, burger patties, great strings of sausage, crates of beer and paper bags of charcoal.

"Junior!" He shouted. "Get out here help the old man."

He looked right into the camera then, his eyes went wide and his jaw dropped so the camera could see right to the back of his pink throat.

The creature knocked the SUV skidding and spraying crushed seashells from under each tire. Wayne stood still, holding a crate of beer under each arm, stain spreading on the front of his jeans.

It rushed him then, knocking him six feet back toward the house. The bottles smashed and rivulets of beer ran along the deck. He tried to crawl away but it stood over him. The camera dipped down toward his legs and there was a wet and crunching snap as it bit into his groin.

He screamed in raw agony and terror, punching feebly as it ragged him from side to side, drawing fans in the gravel to the bare earth below. His outstretched hand was visible for a moment, fingernails ripped off and bloody from trying to cling to the ground as it pulled him. He must have read somewhere that he had to play dead, because he closed his eyes and clamped his mouth shut, shaking with the effort of not screaming.

The camera dipped again. The screen stayed black for a while. Another slow crunch. His scream sounded wrong. When the camera lifted his face was completely demolished, one molar exposed to the root lay on his throbbing neck. One more bite and arterial blood splashed out onto the ground.

A woman's hysterical screaming became obvious then, though it had a scratchy quality that suggested she'd been doing it for a long while. The animal looked to her, attracted by the noise. She was framed in the front door of the house, Mary-Anne Dunbar, professional tennis coach, ten years younger than her husband. She ducked back inside, reappeared a few moments later, a beautiful and ferocious woman, wearing a sundress and hefting a Ruger bolt-action hunting rifle.

The crack of the shot made the microphone distort and she fell backwards against the screen door, shocked by the recoil. The animal jerked, blood spattered the porch steps. She worked the bolt as though she had all the time in the world.

"Fuck you," she screamed, firing again.

This time a thick glob of blood splashed onto the camera lens, a streak and a dot like a semi-colon.

She was working the bolt again when it slammed into her, sending her sailing back into the stairs. The camera was jammed looking through into the dining room as the creature pressed its weight forward onto her, growling and snapping as she screamed for her children.

"Get out, get out, get out!"

There was a rending, twisting sound of gristle, one last low moan and then blood waterfalled down the steps, beading on the entrance hall rug.

The creature stood up straight and turned. There was a flash of something in the mirror over the fireplace, too quick to make out. A strange burst of feedback on the speakers, like a hundred people all screaming high and wounded. The animal seemed far too tall, the camera too high up, twelve, maybe fifteen feet.

The camera slid back down until it was pointing at the staircase. Time enough to see Mary-Anne's twisted head, jaw dislocated, bones pushed up through the skin, one eye gone. Then up to see the little girl crouched at the top of the stairs. Alicia Dunbar, seven years old, freshly bathed, hair combed, clutching a stuffed turtle the newspapers say was called *Señor Tortuga*.

Detective Jackson slapped his palm flat over the center of the screen, used his other hand to turn off the volume on the speaker, and jerked his arm so he could see his Casio wristwatch.

The three men sat in silence for what felt like an awfully long time, as flashes of juddering movement and reddish light leaked from behind his fingers. When he judged that it was over he lifted his hand. The thing was on the landing now, tufts of wet blonde hair wafting before the camera lens tricking out the focus.

The banister rails splintered and cracked as it moved, forcing its huge body down the corridor, heading unerringly through the upper floor, ignoring the closed doors until it came to one at the far back of the house. It burst through, bulging the door off its hinges and shattering the frame.

A teenage boy looked up from where he knelt in the middle of the floor, Wayne Dunbar Jnr. He was a wannabe goth, with eyeliner, nose rings, black nail polish and a death metal t-shirt with a band logo of lightning so squiggly it couldn't be read.

There was a two-thirds empty Morton salt package on the unmade divan. The salt poured out of it into a sloppy circle on the bare boards of the floor. Inside the circle was an eleven-pointed star drawn in neon pink chalk by an unsteady hand. Costco tealight candles stood at each of the points and everywhere the lines of the star intersected. At his feet, an Egyptian-looking knife from a prop store and a wand that probably came from a kid's *One Hundred and One Magic Tricks to Astound Your Friends* kind of set. There was a lizard of some kind, writhing around a yellow thumbtack shoved into its chest bone.

Lusk leant across the screen and paused the video.

"You're a fish and game expert, right?" He asked, laying an evidence baggy on the desk beside the keyboard.

Inside was the malformed lizard from the video, thumbtack still sticking from it. Only it looked a century old, mummified and desiccated almost to the point of dust. It had no head, nor anywhere a head could have been, it was as though the tail ends of four iguanas had been fused together. There was no obvious suture mark or anywhere else it could have been joined. Eight legs. Four tails. Sucker rings all over it like octopus tentacles.

"I've never seen anything like that in my life," the doctor said.

"You and the leading herpetologists in the land both," Jackson said, hitting play.

Onscreen the animal hesitated, pacing from left to right, looking for a way to the kid, like a zoo-bound tiger walking the perimeter of its cage working out how to pounce on the tourist.

Junior panicked then; one of the candles burnt the trailing edge of his bathrobe and he kicked his feet to put it out, smearing the star and circle in the process.

The animal grabbed him at once, biting into his arm and pulling him pleading and screaming down the stairs, past the wreckage of the landing, past the corpses of his family and away into the woods.

"So what do you think?" Lusk asked, stopping the video again.

"Gentlemen, I'm not going to be able to tell you what that thing is," he began, and both detective's shoulders sank as though they'd hoped he could make it make sense where nobody else had been able to. "I can tell you what it's not. Though I think you already know or you never would have called me."

"Get her said." Jackson coughed once more into the tissue, a painful sound.

"Way it moved. Way it attacked. The ferocity of it. Even a pissed off, rabid, one thousand pound grizzly…he doesn't have it in him. But you didn't bring me to talk about the bear, did you, not really?"

"What, uh, what makes you say that?" Lusk asked.

"No, you boys brought me here to talk about the book," the doctor said, and then, seeing the deadpan looks settling over their faces he knew he was right. "You probably know aside from being a fish and game man, I'm a scholar of occult literature, and you hoped I might watch this without saying anything so you could write it off. Despite Junior's appearance as some shit-between-the-ears punk, I got to tell you, he'd got his hands on the occult equivalent of weapons-grade plutonium. The LVV."

"The what now?" Jackson asked, lighting up a cigarette despite the *No Smoking* sign on the wall and another round of coughing.

The doctor rewound the video frame by frame so the creature dragged the boy back up the stairs into his bedroom and pushed him by the arm into the center of the circle. Then he tapped his finger on a book by the boy's feet. It was a hardback with a verdigris-coated brass spine, a rusted chain loop where it had been cut from a lectern. The leather of the binding was so dark green as to be almost black. The only part of it that looked fresh were the letters *LVV* branded into the skin.

"The *Liber Vorpentis Vastitatis*. There's a few ways to translate that. *Book of the Howling Void*. *Book of the Screaming Wastes*. I've been looking into this stuff professionally for near forty years gone. I'm not bragging when I say I have contacts all over the world plugged into the occult underground, and not only have I never seen a copy, I've never met anybody who met anybody who saw a copy.

The best we have is a taxonomic description of the book from 1589, when Dr. John Dee returned to London to find his library looted."

"Who?" Lusk asked, getting out his notebook like he was planning to pull this John Dee in for questioning.

"It's very rare to meet somebody who even knows about it, and those that do tend to keep their mouths shut. Reading the book or even looking at the pictures is supposed to be mind altering."

"So you believe all this shit?" Lusk asked. "No offense."

"Believe? I don't know, but I've seen things I couldn't explain. Things I wouldn't want to go into on the record," the doctor said. The detectives gave each other a look, eyebrows raised. "You boys think what you want about me, I'm too old to give two shits if you wanna call me a crackpot."

He got up to leave and Jackson tapped him on the chest, lowering him gently back into he chair.

"It's not that. We made a decision, long time before you got here, not to show you the rest of the tape. Based on what you just said, and assuming my partner agrees, we've changed our mind."

Jackson skipped forward a few minutes and hit play.

Junior hung down to the left of the camera, arm trailing up off the top of the shot, dangling like a ragdoll. His throat was bitten through so the spine was visible. He should have been dead three times over but he was still breathing, and blood jetted out of the wound into his mouth and nose, choking him.

The animal stood up once more, turning to show a clearing in the trees. The trees bent over backwards away from the center, growing in strange, almost humanoid shapes. The whuffing breaths stopped, there was a spray of colored lights, like grains of molten metal. Then the creature rushed upwards into the air, carrying Junior and the camera with it. It flew up and up until the whole forest spread out below it. There was no city in the distance. No lights. Then the camera fell, plummeting back to the earth where the lens shattered against the floor and all was darkness.

"What do you suppose that means?" Jackson asked.

The doctor could only sit there, mouth gaping, dumbfounded.

"Alright, I'm showing him the other thing," Lusk said, though he didn't make a move until Jackson nodded his approval.

"What other thing?" The doctor asked.

"I was watching your face the whole time. You saw something in the mirror, right, in the house?" Lusk closed the video down, dug deep into another folder and opened another file. "We did too. We had the video tech clean it up for us."

Lusk tapped a few keys and the video played. It was the mirror, zoomed in, enhanced and stabilized.

"Tell me what you see," Jackson said, notebook out, the tip of his tongue protruding onto his lower lip. Cough forgotten.

"It's just the house, reflecting the coach, the bottom of the stairs...the... What the hell is that?"

"Describe it," Jackson said.

"Like, like stars, a starfield, only white instead of black and the stars are...I don't know, globes of darkness. The way, oh fuck, the way they move, they shouldn't, I don't want to...turn it off."

"You're the seventh person to see it," Lusk said. "Everybody sees something different. I saw the inside of a passenger jet, full of naked men and women, all races, all ages, covered in wounds, sitting in their own filth and chained to their seats, averting their eyes from whatever was patrolling up the center aisle. Jackson here saw the—"

"He doesn't need to know that," Jackson said. "There's a woman, name of Special Agent Megan Arliss coming to pick it up tomorrow. Video. Reports. Physical evidence. All of it. Nobody told us which agency and nobody told us on whose authority she's taking over our case. So we didn't feel obliged to tell her we have the book."

"You have it?" the doctor almost jumped up.

"Why, you want to see it?"

"Have any of you looked at it yet?" the doctor asked instead of answering.

"Wagner did," Jackson said. "Right before she took her personal time."

"Anybody checked in on her lately?" The doctor asked.

"No,"

"You should."

Jackson took out his phone and dialed a number. It rang and rang without anybody picking up.

"So you wanna see it or not?" Lusk asked.

"More than anything else in the world," he said, and then when Lusk stood up to go get it from wherever it was kept, added: "And that's why you're not going to let me. You're going to get rid of it. And I don't mean stick it in a trash or trying to burn it. What I'd do, if I had this problem, I'd wrap it in chains, row out to the middle of Tally Lake and dump it overboard. Before you do that, remember though, these things have a way of being found when they want to be."

"You mean the book's alive?" Lusk snorted.

"It ain't a book, it only looks like one,"

"If it's not a book, what the hell is it?"

"A hole."

"A hole in what?"

"Most everything."

The doctor got up to go. Jackson walked him down, leaving Lusk to watch the video for what could have been the thousandth time. The stars were out by the time they got to the parking lot. Jackson's phone was still ringing in his hand, still nobody was picking up.

The doctor got into his car and Jackson leaned in just before he closed the door.

"It was the tumor, in my lung," he said.

"What was?"

"What I saw, in the mirror."

"Why'd you tell me that?"

"I don't know."

The phone finally quit ringing, though not because anybody answered.

The doctor drove away. He looked up into the rearview to see if Jackson was still watching him from the curb. Instead he saw a vast, dead white starfield and black orbs, writhing.

RHIANNON A GRIST
"FOR YOUR CONSIDERATION"

Rhiannon A Grist is an award-winning Welsh writer of weird, dark and speculative fiction. Her Welsh folk horror / dark fantasy novella THE QUEEN OF THE HIGH FIELDS won Best Novella at the 2023 British Fantasy Awards. She lives in Edinburgh with her partner and far too many plants.

Watch out for her debut novel HOME SICK in 2026.

Website: rhiannongrist.wordpress.com
Twitter: @RhiannonAGrist
Bluesky: @RhiannonAGrist
Instagram: @rarrmageddongrist

PETER ROSCH
"EMANCIPATION"

Peter Rosch is the author of *My Dead Friend Sarah, But I Love You, Future Skinny, What The Dead Can Do* (coming Fall 2025 from Crooked Lane Books), and other dark fictions, many born from the addictions he chased while living in New York City. He's sober now but remains an addict's addict: he can turn anything fun into a serious problem.

Website: Peterrosch.com
Bluesky: @peterrosch.bsky.social
Twitter: @PeterRosch
Instagram: @PeterRosch
Threads: @PeterRosch

CALEB BETHEA
"CLOWN SHOWER"

Caleb Bethea is the author of *DISCO MURDER CITY* (Maudlin House '25). Follow along to get *DISCO MURDERED* at CalebBethea.com.

Website: CalebBethea.com
Bluesky: @calebbethea.bsky.social
Twitter: @caleb_bethea_

SOON JONES
"TO WITNESS"

Soon Jones is a second-generation Korean American raised in the rural countryside of the American South. Writing traumatized, feral lesbians is like their whole thing. They are a multi-genre writer and poet, a 2017 Lambda Literary Fellow, and an MFA Poetry candidate at Oklahoma State University. An avid reader and gamer, they spent most of their childhood wandering the deep woods without a path or compass, but always found their way home.

Website: Soonjones.com
Instagram: @thesoonjones
Twitter: @thesoonjones

LAURA KEATING
"DAS WEIBCHEN JEDER TIERART"

Laura Keating is a horror writer from St. Andrews, New Brunswick. She is the author of Agony's Lodestone and The Truest Sense: A Collection of Horror. Her short fiction has been published by Grindhouse Press, Cemetery Gates, Ghost Orchid Press, amongst others. She lives in south shore Nova Scotia with her husband and son. For more information and writing updates, please follow her on Twitter, Instagram, and TikTok @lorekeating or go to her website www.lorekeating.com

Website: Lorekeating.com
Bluesky: @lorekeating.bsky.social
Twitter: @lorekeating
Instagram: @lorekeating

ELOU CARROLL
"EMILY BUYS LOT 1806: A 19TH CENTURY PHOTO ALBUM WITH INSCRIPTION, ALTHOUGH SHE DOESN'T MEAN TO"

Elou Carroll is a graphic designer and freelance photographer who writes. Her work appears or is forthcoming in The Deadlands, Baffling Magazine, If There's Anyone Left (Volume 3), In Somnio: A Collection of Modern Gothic Horror (Tenebrous Press), Spirit Machine (Air and Nothingness Press), Ghostlore (Alternative Stories Podcast) and others. When she's not whispering with ghosts, she can be found editing Crow & Cross Keys, publishing all things dark and lovely, and spending far too much time on twitter (@keychild). She keeps a catalogue of her weird little wordcreatures on www.eloucarroll.com.

Website: Eloucarroll.com
Bluesky: @keychild.bsky.social
Twitter: @keychild

ARISTO COUVARAS
"COOKING_ALONE@NIGHT"

Aristo Couvaras was born to Greek parents in Durban, South Africa. He attended the University of the Witwatersrand, where he obtained a Bachelor of Arts, as well as a Bachelor of Laws. Aristo and his wife live on the island of Cyprus.

His stories have been featured in *Found: An Anthology of Found Footage Horror Stories*, Timber Ghost Press' *Along Harrowed Trails*, at horrortree.com, Econoclash Review, Things in the Well's anthologies, *Beneath the Waves - Tales from the Deep* and *Trickster's Treats 4*, Critical Blast's anthology, *Gods & Services*, Fantasia Divinity's *Behind Glass Eyes*, Macabre Ladies' Dark Carnival and Media Macabre's *The Little Book of Cursed Dolls*.

Aristo can be found on Twitter **@AR1sto.**

LINDA B ADAMS
"DIGGING FOR THE DISAPPEARED"

Linda B. Adams is a writer, photographer, and urban explorer living in Northern New York. She is a member of the Horror Writers Association and has served as a juror for the Bram Stoker Awards. She has an MA in English and has taught fiction and memoir workshops through Poets & Writers. Her fiction and photography have appeared in Rock and A Hard Place Magazine. She lives with her two rescue cats, far too many clown figures, and a mountainous TBR pile.

Twitter: @lindabwriter
Bluesky: @lindabwriter.bsky.social

STEVE LOIACONI
"TRANSCRIPTS OF SANDWICH REVIEWS POSTED BY DOMINIC STACHOWSKI BEFORE THE MURDERS"

Steve Loiaconi is a journalist and a graduate of George Mason University's MFA program. His fiction previously appeared in Griffel, the Mystery Tribune, Allegory, Mythaxis, and the Saturday Evening Post, as well as the anthologies Dracula's Guests, Open All Night, and Why Didn't You Just Leave. He lives in Washington, DC with his wife, son, and dog.

Website: steveloiaconi.wordpress.com
Bluesky: @sloiaconi.bsky.social
Twitter: @sloiaconi

C.J. DOTSON
"A PLACE WHERE THE SUN HAS NEVER SHONE"

C.J. Dotson possesses the statistically average number of body parts for a human being to have. She and her husband, stepson, and children (all of whom also appear human) share a cabin in the woods with more bugs than she would ever like to see.

Her "heart hammering, breath shuddering" (Cynthia Pelayo, Bram Stoker Award-winning author of *Forgotten Sisters*) debut horror novel THE CUT comes out April 8th, 2025 from Macmillan Publishers.

In her limited spare time she enjoys reading, video games, painting, baking and decorating cakes (with…questionable success), and petting her puppy and three cats.

Website: cjdotsonauthor.com
Bluesky: @cj-dotson.bsky.social
Twitter: @cj_dots

JASON FISCHER
"BORROWED TIME"

Jason Fischer is a horror and crime author specializing in short stories. His work has appeared in numerous magazines and anthologies, including A Hint of Hitchcock, Halloween Horrors–13 Tales of Terror, Manor of Frights, and Inanimate Things. His short story collection, The Haunting of Towne Point Mall -10 Interconnected Tales of Psychological Terror, will be published by Velox Books in 2025. When not writing, you can find Jason biking the trails around his home, playing with his nephews, adding to his VHS collection, or on the deck feeding the deer and enjoying nature.

Website: jasonfischerauthor.com
Twitter: @jhorror73
Facebook: https://www.facebook.com/jasonfischerh orror

KATHY M. BATES
"DOPPELGÄNGER"

Kathy M. Bates is a writer, gamer, and sometimes adjunct professor living in the southern United States. She received her MFA in creative writing from the University of Central Arkansas. Her work has appeared in the Mid/South Anthology from Belle Point Press, JMWW, Arkana, Necessary Fiction, and elsewhere.

Website: kmbates.com
Bluesky: @hellokmbates.bsky.social
Twitter: @HelloKMBates
Instagram: @HelloKMBates

ANGELA SYLVAINE
"A KING IS NOTHING WITHOUT HIS QUEEN"

Angela Sylvaine is a self-proclaimed cheerful goth who writes speculative fiction and poetry. Horror-comedy fans enjoy her novel, Frost Bite, a '90s sci-fi horror comedy, and her retro 80s YA mall slasher novella, Chopping Spree. For sad girl horror, check out her debut short story collection, The Dead Spot: Stories of Lost Girls. Her short fiction and poetry have appeared in or on over fifty anthologies, magazines, and podcasts, including Southwest Review, Apex, and The NoSleep Podcast. She lives in the shadow of the Rocky Mountains with her sweetheart and three creepy cats.

Website: angelasylvaine.com.
Bluesky: @angelasylvaine.bsky.social
Twitter: @sylvaine_angela
Instagram: @angela_sylvaine/

E.S. HUBERTY
"MOTHER OF BLOOD"

E.S. Huberty (she/her) is a freelance writer living near Portland, Oregon. Her short fiction has been published by Hungry Shadow Press and Bag of Bones Press, among other places. When not writing, she enjoys video games, baking, and hiking.

Bluesky: @eshuberty.bsky.social
Instagram: @eshuberty91

D.A. JOBE
"A METEOROLOGICAL HISTORY OF CRYSTAL CLOUD ELDENA"

D. A. Jobe is a Virginia writer with a love of music, traveling,and horror movies. Her short stories appear in Monstrous Futures: A Sci-Fi Horror Anthology (2023, Dark Matter INK) and Bodies Full of Burning: An Anthology of Menopause-themed Horror (2020, Sliced Up Press). Her novel, PALMETTO BOY, is slated for publication by Timber Ghost Press in 2026.

Website: dajobeauthor@wordpress.com
Bluesky: @d-a-jobe.bsky.social
Twitter: @D_A_Jobe

AMANDA M. BLAKE
"NUISANCE NOTIFICATIONS"

A mass of tentacles and rose vines masquerading as a person, **Amanda M. Blake** is the author of such horror titles as QUESTION NOT MY SALT, DEEP DOWN, and OUT OF CURIOSITY AND HUNGER, dark poetry collection DEAD ENDS, and the Thorns fairy tale mash-up series.

Website: amandamblake.com
Bluesky: @amandamblake.bsky.social
Twitter: @AmandaMBlake1

CHRIS PANATIER
"TO THE ATTENTION OF GERALDO"

Chris Panatier lives in Dallas, Texas, with his wife, daughter, and a fluctuating herd of animals resembling dogs. He writes short stories and novels, and draws album covers for metal bands.

Website: www.chrispanatier.com
Bluesky: @scribeofhades.bsky.social
Twitter: @chrisjpanatier
Instagram: @chrispanatier

MATTHEW J. HOCKEY
"TRAIL CAM 004"

Matthew J. Hockey recently relocated his family from Northern England to Southern Spain for reasons that should be obvious to anybody who's ever been to either of those places. His short horror and weird stories and flash fiction have appeared in print and online since 2015. His latest story 'Ad Infinitum' will be part of Songs from the Void coming from Max Blood Publications in 2025.

Bluesky: @mathockey.bsky.social
Twitter: @MatthewHockey1

ANDREW CULL
Editor

Andrew Cull is an award-winning writer and horror director. He's the author of *Bones*, *Remains*, and, most recently, *The Cockroach King*. His story collection *Bones* has been described as "a masterclass in emotional cinematic horror fiction."

His new novella, *She Says Die* is coming at you with teeth bared and a loaded shotgun in 2025.

Andrew lives in Melbourne, Australia. He loves horror and Hitchcock, and, like you, he's not easily scared.

Instagram: @andrew_cull
Bluesky: @andrewcull.bsky.social
Twitter: @andrewcull.

GABINO IGLESIAS
Editor

Gabino Iglesias is a writer, journalist, professor, and literary critic living in Austin, TX. He is also the author of the critically acclaimed and award-winning novels *House of Bone and Rain*, *The Devil Takes You Home*, *Zero Saints* and *Coyote Songs*.

Iglesias' nonfiction has appeared in the *New York Times*, the *Los Angeles Times*, *Electric Literature*, and *LitReactor*, and his reviews appear regularly in places like *NPR*, *Publishers Weekly*, *the San Francisco Chronicle*, *the Boston Globe*, *Criminal Element*, *Mystery Tribune*, *Vol. 1 Brooklyn*, and *the Los Angeles Review of Books*.

He's been a juror for the *Shirley Jackson Awards* twice and the *Millions* Tournament of Books, and is a member of the Horror Writers Association, the Mystery Writers of America, and the National Book Critics Circle.

Follow Gabino on Twitter: @Gabino_Iglesias.

FOUND

An Anthology of Found Footage Horror Stories.

Between April and August 2021 eighteen horror writers disappeared. Gathered together for the first time, these are the stories they were writing at the time of their disappearances.

Stories by: Holly Rae Garcia, Jeremy Hepler, Bev Vincent, Ally Wilkes, Clay McLoed Chapman, Nick Kolakowski, Tim McGregor, Alan Baxter, Angela Sylvaine, Josh Rountree, Georgia Cook, Ali Seay, Donna Lynch, Kurt Fawver, Robert Levy, Joe Butler, Fred Fischer IV, Aristo Couvaras.

Reader caution is advised. Advance readers of this anthology have reported nausea, feelings of anxiety, paranoia and hallucinations after reading the texts included.

OBSERVATIONS.

Error: message function (please fill out all fields?)

OBSERVATIONS.

<u>NOTES ~~not OBS~~.</u>

Can you hear it ~~listening~~ while you sleep?
Hahaahahaahahahahahahahahahahaha

CRIESCRIESCRIES ~~NOTES~~ not ~~OBS~~.

SCRIESSCRIESSCRIES ~~NOTES~~ not ~~OBS~~.

~~You'll see it soon~~

<u>THANKYOUFORREADING**GLISTENING**UINEAPIG</u>

L
I
S
T
E
N
I
N
G
W
O
R
D
S

F
F
#
3
1
0
,
2
6

B
Y
E